Artifacts & Amulets

A Paranormal Witch Cozy Mystery

Book Store Cozy Mystery Series
Book 8

Lucinda Race

MC Two Press

Editor: Trish Long
Cover design by Mariah Sinclair

Manufactured in the United States of America
First Edition August 2024

Print Edition ISBN 978-1-954520-82-0
E-book ISBN 978-1-954520-81-3

Pembroke Cove, ME

1. Robin's Cafe
2. Bygone Antiques
3. The Pembroke Cliffs
4. Cozy Nook Bookstore
5. Twisted Scissors Hair Salon
6. Betty's Market
7. Old Town Library
8. Miss Judy's Dance Studio
9. The Sweet Spot Baker
10. Bee Bee's Boutique
11. Tuckers Hardware Store
12. The Copper Kettle
13. Police Station
14. Town Hall

Chapter 1
Lily

Q UICK NOTE: If you enjoy Artifacts & Amulets, be sure to check out my offer for a FREE novella at the end. With that, happy reading.

***

The door to the Cozy Nook Bookshop opened with a sharp bang. A man, about fifty, with streaks of gray in his hair and mustache, scowled at me. He wore a crisp brown suit with a white shirt and orange tie that reminded me of a pumpkin. The woman was a bit younger, wearing a dark skirt, matching jacket, and a pale blue blouse, making her deep blue eyes more pronounced, and three-inch heels. Her hair was coiffed in a short, no-nonsense style that complimented her face. She closed the door and glanced around, her face expressionless.

"Welcome to my bookstore. I'm Lily. If there is anything I can help you find, please ask."

The man gave a curt nod of acknowledgment as the woman stepped to the counter. I was perched on a wooden stool and put aside my family's book on magic, *Practical Beginnings*, that I had been reading.

"Is there a specific book you're looking for today?"

She glanced at the man and back at me. "I am. A book on amulets. Do you have anything in stock?"

I gave her a wide smile. "Yes." I stood and headed down the aisle close to where my familiar, Milo, was snoozing on the window seat. The sun streamed in the large plate glass windows, bathing his gray fur in warmth. He lifted his head and looked at the customer through slits in his eyes before he bolted to an upright position.

I smiled at the couple. "Did you know there is an exhibit at the Olde Town Library with artifacts that include several amulets? Their history is reported to be quite interesting."

The man said, "Why do you think we're in town? We forgot our reference books in the city, so show us what you have and stop jaw-jacking."

I didn't appreciate his cantankerous tone, but the old saying the customer is always right had me tamping down a sharp retort. I gestured to the shelf in front of them as if we were on a game show and I was the hostess showing off the gifts. "Here you go. As you can see, there are several. I hope you find what you're looking for."

The woman tipped her head. "Thank you."

She turned her back to me as if I shouldn't see what book she picked up first. I took the hint that I was dismissed and took my time going back to the counter. The couple didn't seem to be enjoying their day, and I found this curious. Outside, the sun was bright; temperatures were pleasant for a June day, and from what I had heard, the exhibit at the library was fascinating. I caught Milo staring at me, and I gave him a wink. If he wanted to talk to me, he could, non-magicals would only hear him meow. He hopped to the floor, leaving one of his favorite napping spots, and trotted behind me. I picked him up and set him on the counter.

While Milo and I waited, the woman's voice was laced with agitation. "I must see the Heart of the Soul amulet. It is imperative my proposal is accepted."

Nodding in their direction, I whispered, "What do you think their problem is?"

In a deep kitty growl, Milo said, "Be careful. I'll explain later."

I was surprised to see him continue to stare in the customers' direction. He was engrossed by their conversation. I arched a brow in his direction, but he ignored me and swished his tail in a jerky side-to-side motion.

After several long minutes, the couple carried a stack of books to the desk. The woman sorted through the titles, handing five to the man and placing one on the table behind them. With a thud, he set them on the counter next to Milo. "We'll take these."

"If you need directions to the library, it's on the corner of Doenut Drive and Route 1 on the right, at the end. But if you'd prefer to walk, you can cut through the town square and get there in a few minutes."

"Good to know."

I rang up the books and gave him the total, but the woman handed me her credit card. I glanced at the name as the transaction was being processed. "Petra. That's a beautiful name."

"Dr. Addington." She wrenched the card from my hands. "Can I sign for the purchase please?"

My eyes widened at her rudeness, but she wouldn't be the last customer with an attitude when they entered my shop. As I slipped her books into a brown paper bag, I looked past her to see what the man was doing.

He was reading the back jacket of the book Petra had set aside.

"Simon. The bag." Without so much as a thank you, she turned in her pumps and strode to the door, her heels clacking against the wood floor.

The man, who I now knew as Simon, shrugged. "The boss." He trailed after her, looking more like a sad puppy than a grown man.

The door closed with much less force than when it was opened, and I watched Petra and Simon get into a heated exchange. Petra's arms were flailing about, and she repeatedly jabbed him in the middle of his chest. He stepped back while she advanced on him, still carrying on. I wished the windows were open to hear what they were saying.

"You know, my dear witch, if you hadn't been slacking on your studies, you might have discovered the spell for eavesdropping. Typically, it's frowned upon in our coven. However, there are circumstances in which rules could be interpreted that it was warranted, especially when it's easy to see she is extremely agitated." He tipped his head back and watched me, watching the action outside.

"What do you know about the Heart of the Soul? I've never heard of it."

"It's an amulet." He quickly jumped to the floor and trotted into the back room.

That short answer wasn't like Milo. "Where are you going?"

"Out." He pushed on the kitty door and left it swinging in his wake.

I crossed my arms over my chest and then looked at the sidewalk. Petra and Simon were gone. If I hadn't been distracted, I could have seen in which direction they went. Glancing at the desk calendar, I was pleased to realize the library was open late tonight. With a quick text to my fiancé, Detective Gage Erikson of the Pembroke Police Department, I let him know I'd be stopping at the library after I closed the store. I smiled at the idea of spending time at the library in spite of Milo's rude departure.

What was it today with rudeness? I sank to the stool. My eyes were drawn to the kitty door. Where had he gone?

I placed my hand on the old leather-bound book in front of me and closed my eyes. I focused on Milo, and the cover warmed under my touch. The tug of concern to make sure my familiar was safe increased. I opened the book. Pages began to turn, first right and then left until it lay open. I read the title of the spell; *Stay Connected to Your Familiar*. This was just what I needed. I continued to read aloud. *To create a deeper connection between a witch and her familiar, recite this spell.* Under my breath I said:

> Two peas in a pod are we.
> For when I need to see what you can see.
> Not to be used frivolously.
> This I wish and so it shall be.

After I had read through it once, I read it out loud again with more conviction in my voice. I crossed to the front window and looked across the town square, hoping to catch a glimpse of my gray fur ball. But he was nowhere to be seen. I was tempted to use the summoning spell. Instead, I closed my eyes and repeated the connection spell again. This time, I could see the front doors of the library from the elevation of the sidewalk. Was it possible I could see what Milo saw at this very moment?

In my vision I saw a leaf skitter across the sidewalk, but the focus on the front doors never wavered. He knew how to get inside if that was what he wanted. I waited another couple of minutes before I opened my eyes. The urge to know what was going on was stronger than before. For now, I'd bide my time. In a moment of clarity, I decided Milo would go with me to the library tonight. There was more than one way to get to the bottom of things.

An hour later, Milo slunk around a bookcase. I watched him out of the corner of my eye as he paused and then sat down. "My dear witch, can we talk?"

"Always." I gestured to the wingback chairs positioned near the front window. It was one of my favorite places to curl up. Often, I enjoyed a hot beverage and read when time permitted or shared coffee and a sweet treat with Gage or whoever else might stop in.

With a tentative gait, he walked to one of the chairs and jumped up. A band constricted my heart. Whatever was going on with Milo had me on edge. He never moved at a sedate pace. I sat next to him and folded my hands in my lap. "I'm ready whenever you are."

He tipped his head down as if the fabric on the chair was the most important thing he needed to see. I wasn't about to push him to open up. After my family's book of witchcraft clonked me on the head almost a year ago and I discovered my rescue cat could talk, I learned patience was the key to good communication with Milo.

"Have you ever wondered how I became a familiar?"

His normal snarky kitty growl was absent, and he sounded as if he had lost his only friend. I knew I was about to say something stupid, but I had to ask. "You weren't born a familiar?"

He lifted his head and glared at me. "Familiars aren't born. We're made from other beings such as a witch or wizard."

"Oh." What was I expected to say and how would I have known? Should I have thought to ask when I learned the truth about myself and him? "What were you, a witch?"

His nod was barely noticeable. As he began to speak, I leaned closer so as not to miss a single word. "It was a long time ago, and I was respected as a fair and honorable witch. But some craved the power I possessed. You see, as a young witch, I discovered the rarest red opal anyone had ever seen. I had crafted an amulet and imbued it with a spell that as long as I wore it, my powers would remain pure and strong. As the years went by, I grew complacent. I let my guard down. A witch joined our coven in the neighboring village. There were whispers, but I let arrogance cloud my judgement. She wanted to claim the amulet I wore around my neck for herself. With trickery, she got my amulet and cursed me to life as a familiar. Before her spell changed the course of my life, I was able to change the course of hers. I cursed the amulet that whoever should wear it, if they had an impure heart, would perish."

My hand flew to my mouth. "Milo, you cast a death curse?"

"Yes, and you deserve to know the truth before I leave. I did the unforgivable."

"Did the witch who took your amulet..." I didn't want to say the words, and thank the stars Milo didn't wait for me to finish my question.

"Yes. She died. It was such a chaotic time in our town. The power struggles between good witches and evil. A tale as old as time. There were rumors, of course, about the amulet, but I lost track of it. Now, this beautiful, cursed object is part of a traveling exhibit and should never fall into the wrong hands." He lay down and covered his head with his paws in shame.

Why was he telling me this now? And I quickly rewound the events from earlier. "Milo."

When he didn't pick his head up, I scooped him from the chair. After placing a tender kiss on the middle of his head and holding him away from my body so I could see into his deep green eyes. "Milo, what was the name of your amulet?" My heart thudded in my chest. I knew before he would tell me, but I had to hear it from him.

"The amulet of Aathmika."

"And you're Aathmika." There was no need for the question. I just needed confirmation. "What does that mean?"

"Once upon a time, I was. It means soulful and close to

the inner heart." He hung his head. "Now, instead of being a powerful witch, I am a humble teacher for you, my dear witch."

I crushed him to my chest and blinked the tears from my eyes. "Your amulet is in our library."

"Yes, and I can tell you that woman who was here plans to steal it."

"Petra Addington? How do you know that?"

"Guess." He squirmed from my arms and dropped to the floor. "I followed them and heard what they were saying. Non-magical people never pay attention to a cat when they're talking." He ran his paw over one side of his whiskers. "For the record, Simon was still arguing with her. He said she was being foolish. There was no way she would get her hands on it." He grumbled, "Heart of the Soul. You have to ask yourself who renamed that to make it sound sweet and innocent."

"Well, it's based on facts. You said it means soul and inner heart. At some point, the name was changed." I got to my feet. "I texted Gage, and we're meeting at the library. Do you want to come with us or stay here?"

Milo's body shook from the tips of his whiskers to the end of his tail. "I don't know that I want to see it. After all this time, it still might be too painful. A reminder of all that I've lost."

I knelt on the floor and ran my hand over the length of his soft fur. "Milo, you won't be alone. I'll be with you. And whatever happened all those years ago can't hurt you again."

He leaned into my hand. "Lily, you'll need to do some recon work and confirm the curse is still as strong as ever.

The amulet must be protected at all costs. If it falls into the wrong hands, I shudder to think what might happen, especially if it's a non-magical. That screams disaster."

"How can I do that short of putting the amulet on? Which, for the record, I don't even want to think about doing. Should I have Dax come with Gage?"

"First, you're a Michaels witch and pure of heart. I don't think it could hurt you." Milo nodded when I mentioned a more seasoned witch to accompany us. Gage was a non-magical, and I was still new at a lot of witchy stuff.

"Asking Detective Sweet Tea to join us might not be a bad idea. Dax Peters is more than competent; his powers are off the charts. But why don't you ask them to come by here first, and I can fill them in on the high-level curse information? I wouldn't want your Detective Cutie to try and touch it. There's no way to know just how strong the magic is."

I loved that Milo had given them both nicknames. Gage was really good looking, and Dax, being from Louisiana, got the moniker, Sweet Tea, not that he drank much tea; coffee was his beverage of choice. But the names were endearing. I had one lingering question. "Where did you get the name Milo?"

"My familiar gave his life protecting me. It was the best way I knew to honor his sacrifice."

A lump rose in my throat. I made a silent vow. Never put my precious Milo in a position where he'd have to protect me at the cost of putting his own life in peril. I pulled him to my chest and smothered him with kisses.

"Stop." He swatted my cheek with his paw, claw

tucked in. He coughed like he wanted to hack up a small hairball. "Now, what about reading some of the book *Practical Beginnings?* You never know when you might need a new spell."

I gave him a half smile. "Are you kidding? I'm going to start at the beginning and read every single page. If trouble is brewing, I'm going to be prepared."

"First text Gage, and don't forget to ask Detective Sweet Tea to come too." He slipped from my arms and stalked to the window seat. "I need a nap."

He turned around three times and curled into a ball. So much had happened in the last fifteen minutes I felt like I'd been sideswiped with information. My familiar once had been a powerful witch. Didn't my aunt Mimi know, and if she did, why in the heavens and earth hadn't she told me? First things first, text Gage. Then call my aunt.

Chapter 2
Lily

I watched Gage through the front window as he strode across the town square, his long legs closing the distance between us. With a sigh, I leaned against the counter. Dang, he was easy on the eyes. He wore his usual cowboy boots, acid-washed jeans, and dark blue polo with the Pembroke Cove police department emblem. The wind ruffled his short brown hair. I knew behind the dark aviator sunglasses, his hazel eyes were laser focused on my shop. Matching his stride was his best friend and transplant to Pembroke Cove, Dax Peters. Today, he didn't look like a former federal officer from DC. His usual creased black dress pants, black blazer, and white buttoned shirt had been replaced with dark jeans and the same polo shirt Gage wore. Instead of boots, he wore shiny black loafers. This was progress.

The bell above the door jingled when Gage pushed it. Before I could rush over and throw my arms around his neck and kiss him, he had swept me into his arms. With a soul-stirring kiss, it was evident he was happy I had texted him. I looked around him. Dax closed the door and bent over to chat with Milo.

"Hey, Dax. I haven't seen you for a couple of days. How's my brother from another coven?"

He picked up Milo and carried him across the room to join me and Gage. "Busy." He glanced at Gage, his brow furrowed.

It seemed by the look they exchanged, something had happened which I might not like. "What's going on?"

Gage slipped his arm around my waist and said, "You might as well tell her. She'll find out."

Still holding Milo and petting him, Dax said, "I've been offered a job which I'm seriously considering."

My heart sank. Dax had become a trusted friend, a partner in sleuthing, Gage's best friend, and an important part of our group. I didn't want him to move. Everyone knew how things went. You'd promise to keep in touch. In the beginning, everyone made the time. Then slowly, that changed. People stopped putting in the effort and drifted apart.

"I don't want you to go." I looked from Gage to Dax. "Is someone giving you a hard time in the department?"

He chuckled. "Lily, it's not like that. Remember when we worked on Archie Dane's untimely departure from this earth?"

"Yes, that was six months ago." Gage hugged me close to his side before releasing me. I knew he was trying to reassure me.

"I spent some time with the officers in Robins Pointe. A few days ago, I was approached to take over the department."

"Huh?" This was not what I had wanted to talk about.

"They've offered me the position of chief. I'm seriously considering it."

Milo cranked his head in Dax's direction. "I didn't know you were looking for another job."

Neither had I. Bless Milo for saying what I was thinking.

"I wasn't. The current chief said I impressed everyone. When he decided to retire, he approached the town board and tossed my name into the running. I've had a couple of conversations with the board and other officers to see if I'd be a good fit. Today, I was offered the job."

I sagged into a chair. Robins Pointe was only thirty minutes away. I could hear the excitement in his voice, and the way his eyes sparkled, it was easy to see he wanted to say yes. "If this is what you want, why are you thinking about it?"

"Honestly, I've gotten used to living in Pembroke Cove, and to move again in less than a year is a lot to undertake." He gently placed Milo on the floor. "There's a feeling I have, way deep down inside that I can't put into words. I need to take a leap and accept the position. However, I don't want to rush into a decision. I told the board I'd let them know by next Monday."

"That gives you plenty of time to consider every angle and," I wriggled my eyebrows, "we'll pull out my clue board and make a list of pros and cons. It's proven to be an excellent tool as we've tracked down some unsavory characters since you arrived. It's fitting to put it to use for this puzzle."

He chuckled. "And we all know how much you love a puzzle. Even if we don't make a list, I'd like to get together for dinner tonight at the Clam Bake and talk it over. You're my best friends, and I value your input."

Gage smiled. "Spoken like a native. All important decisions should be made over lobster."

I tapped the tabletop. "That's after we take in the exhibit at the library." My eyes connected with Milo. I needed to share a part of the story he told me but not the part about his connection to one particular piece. That was just between us.

Gage quirked an eyebrow. "What makes this exhibit so hot you need to see it tonight? You haven't mentioned it before."

"I had two customers in today, and they bought some books about amulets. They mentioned that one is stunning and quite significant in its history. The woman, Petra Addington, was very excited to see it in person."

Dax looked from Milo to me, his dark eyes clouded. "What was the name of the amulet?"

"I think she said, Heart of the Soul." I didn't dare glance at Milo. I took deep, steady breaths to control my breathing. I wouldn't let on that I needed to see this particular artifact from my familiar's past. "It's a red opal, and based on the pictures I looked up on the internet, it's stunning."

"What else did the internet tell you?" Dax asked.

I avoided his penetrating gaze and hurried over to my laptop. Turning the screen around so that Gage and Dax could see the necklace, I said, "This article says it's a few hundred years old, and the person who wears it can have bad luck."

Milo coughed. Dax leveled his gaze on him. "Is that all?"

With a shrug, I said, "That's all it says, and you know me; once that couple started talking about it, I grew curious." I closed the laptop and gave Gage and Dax what I hoped was a charming smile. "I'll need a few minutes to lock up in the back, and then we can head over."

I had already prepared to close up, but I wanted to get Milo alone. There were a couple of questions that needed answers before we left. I hurried into the back room to lock the door, and Milo trotted after me. With a glance over my shoulder to reassure myself the guys had stayed put, I tapped the countertop. Milo jumped up with ease.

"Would Dax know about your history?"

"Not me specifically. He would have heard of the witch who once possessed and lost the Amulet of Aathmika and might even have heard its new name. But the only person who knows the full story is you."

A lump bobbed in my throat. "I'm the only person you told? I'm humbled."

Milo touched my hand with his paw. "I trust you with my life just as you do with me. But we have to make sure the amulet is protected. It's in danger. I can feel it in my soul. It must not fall into the hands of that woman who was here today. If it does, it will be very bad. The only reason it exists is to remind all good witches and wizards that magic can be tainted and honor must always be uppermost in your mind."

I had never heard Milo so articulate and adamant about anything. I missed his snark, and the sooner we knew that there was no way Petra Addington or anyone else could get their hands on the amulet, the better.

"What's the plan when we get to the library?"

Milo jumped down from the counter. "We'll react as events unfold."

Gage and I walked hand in hand down the brick sidewalk. Milo trotted in the lead, and Dax was next to me. If the guys thought it was odd Milo was coming, neither of them mentioned it. A few cars were parked in the lot next to the library. I wondered how many people had been through the exhibit since it arrived in town. We climbed the wide stone steps, and Dax pulled open the heavy wooden and glass door, allowing Milo to slip in first, and we followed.

The new head librarian, Paige Reed, was seated at the desk just inside the door and flashed us a welcoming smile. "Hello, have you come to see the amulet exhibit?"

I caught a glimpse of Milo's tail as he slipped through the door to the annex. "We are. Has it been busy? It's not often we get such a rare exhibit in our small town."

"I've been surprised it's very popular. In fact, we've had several people travel from Buffalo to see it. I guess the small library event has been popular. We're lucky Pembroke Cove was one of the few in the Northeast to have this honor." Paige gestured to the entrance. "Go on in. Only a few people are taking the self-guided tour at the moment."

I thanked her, and we followed Milo. To Gage's credit, he never asked why Milo had come. I suspected Dax was curious, but he would wait to see what was happening before he commented.

The room was quiet, with the exception of a hum of reverent whispers as a couple strolled down the aisle in front of us, looking at each amulet and reading the captions out loud. I scanned the left side of the room for Milo. He was nowhere to be seen. I had turned to the right when a few voices were getting louder. I hurried in that direction to discover Petra and her friend Simon were having a heated argument with three people I didn't recognize.

"What are you talking about?" Petra's face was crimson. "This is a red opal."

"Petra calm down." The man gave a pleading look to the two women he was with. "Roni, Donella, tell her that she's right so we can move on."

Simon held out one of the books they had purchased at my shop. "It says right here the Heart of the Soul is an extremely rare red opal."

One of the women spoke, "Donella and I aren't disagreeing about what the base is, but what we're saying is this particular amulet is beautiful but dangerous. It's not bestowed with goodness. A curse waits for the unlucky soul to slip it on. That's why you shouldn't even think about it as anything but something to respect from a distance."

The corner of Petra's lip curled up. "You're jealous that I have been granted special permission to examine it. Late to the party again, Roni." Petra turned her back on the newcomers.

The woman, who I thought was Donella, straightened her spine and flipped her dark hair over her shoulder. "We'll see who ends up publishing the real paper on the authenticity of this priceless jewel. You may be a respected archeologist in our field, but you won't win, Petra. Not this time. I'll see to that."

Roni took a step toward Simon. "You'd best get your boss, the self-important Dr. Addington, to see reason. We should work collaboratively. We've all dreamt of this opportunity." She glanced at the man. "Chaz, let's leave Petra and Simon to their observations. We have some phone calls to make. And Petra, you can be sure this is not the last time we'll discuss the Heart of the Soul." Roni snorted and glared at her took a menacing step closer to the doctor. "Ironic, isn't it? You have neither.

In a single file, the strangers walked out of the annex.

"Petra? Are you alright?" I stopped short when I saw what she was studying intently. Milo's amulet was suspended in the center of the glass case. The light caused the gem to dance with a brilliant fire. The depth of the red and black colors seemed as if it had been recently polished.

"It's beautiful." The words slipped out of me.

Petra glanced in my direction, and a small satisfied smile played over her mouth. "It really is. I've waited a lifetime to get this close to it. This particular piece has been locked away for over fifty years."

"Why so long?"

Gage came up behind me and said, "Is this the necklace you wanted to see?"

A frown replaced Petra's smile. "It's an amulet, please respect it."

"Sorry." Gage said as he slipped his hand in mine. "What's the difference?"

"A necklace is an adornment, but an amulet has powers

beyond your wildest dreams. I only wish I could wear it even for a minute. I could die a happy woman."

"Dr. Addington," Simon said, "don't jest about something that holds dire consequences. With good, it must be balanced with evil."

She waved a dismissive hand in his direction. I noticed the gleam in her eye. "Not to worry Simon, it's not like I'll ever be able to actually touch it. It's in a protective case." She gave me a nod. "Enjoy the exhibit." She snapped her jacket closed, and Simon nodded as he passed us.

As I watched them leave the room, Milo snaked his body around my legs and grumbled, "Things just got interesting."

And I had to agree.

Chapter 3
Gage

Lily's face was devoid of a smile as she scanned the open space as we entered the library. This had always been her happy place. Hosting the monthly movie night was a highlight even after the previous librarian had been killed on the front steps. If I hadn't known her well, I wouldn't have noticed the small jerky movements as she moved to the interior of the annex, where the exhibit was being held. And what was Milo doing? The only time I had known he'd come here was when he was helping Lily get out of the locked building when I was investigating Flora's murder.

Lily was still standing near one of the displays. I didn't understand why the woman with an English accent was going to take a swing at the woman who I thought had been called Roni. Now that the five strangers had left the building I needed to get a closer look at the amulet that was causing such an uproar.

"Sweetheart. Care to fill me in on the backstory of this necklace, I mean amulet?"

She flashed a look at Milo who was sitting at her feet. His tail swished from side to side in a jerky motion.

"I'll give you the highlights. Petra Addington seems to be fixated on it. And I must say it is beautiful. But if the legend is true and it's been cursed, I wonder why she is determined to put her hands on it? Sometimes artifacts from the past should be respected and admired instead of trying to unravel the mystery."

I blinked hard. Was this the Lily Michaels I knew and loved? There was never a puzzle she hadn't wanted to get to the bottom of. She must know more than she was saying, but why hold back from me?

I took a step closer to the glass. "Any idea who donated it or how it came to be a part of this exhibit?"

Dax joined us and gave Lily a quizzical look before saying, "I've heard stories about an amulet that looks very similar. It wasn't called the Heart of the Soul. Seems at one time it belonged to a powerful witch. No one knows for sure what happened to the witch, but his protection amulet fell into the wrong hands. From that point forward, its rumored to have been cursed. Whoever wears it will die."

The color drained from Lily's face. "That's just awful. Can you imagine, as a witch, losing something so valuable?"

Her fingers traced the outline of her amethyst protection necklace. She had worn it every day since her Aunt Mimi gave it to her last year. The color slowly returned to her face as if merely touching it brought her peace.

"No one really believes a piece of jewelry can be cursed. I mean that's in fairy tales." The blank look that passed between Dax and Lily now made my blood chill. "Is there really something to this curse?"

Milo meowed, and Lily picked him up. She rubbed his ears and kept him close to her body. She said, "Yes. The story has been handed down from coven to coven for generations. And it's good that the red opal is safely secured in a case. Sometimes surface beauty can mask the darkness that lingers under the shimmer."

Dax stared at Lily, and Milo tapped her cheek. "Now that we've seen the exhibit, I'll take Milo home and meet you gentlemen at the restaurant."

I was hesitant to point out that we really hadn't experienced all of the artifacts. It was obvious there was much more going on that I wasn't privy to. "I'll follow you home. Then we can ride together to the Clam Shack."

Dax said, "I'm going to look at a few more things, and I'll meet you there in thirty minutes."

Lily dropped her eyes to Milo and said, "Sounds like we have a plan."

Without waiting for me, she hurried out of the room as Milo began to meow. I still wished I could speak familiar, but as a non-magical, it wasn't possible. Even after talking to my mom, who happens to be a witch and part of the local coven, there was no known spell that could help me. I hurried after Lily. I might not understand Milo, but she and I would have a conversation after we dropped him off.

Twenty minutes later, Lily was sitting in the passenger seat of my pickup truck. She twirled the knob on the radio, looking for music and not talk radio while doing her best not to engage in conversation. I could wait. Even if we didn't talk about what had happened in the last hour, I would get the chance at some point tonight.

"Over the last few days, the weather has been nice. Before we know it, the tourists will arrive in droves. Which is always good for the bookstore business." She flashed me a strained smile. "For the police department too, all those parking tickets."

I chuckled. "Leave it to you to see how the town gets extra revenue from tickets." I slowed as we approached the parking area for the Clam Shack. The lot was packed tonight. A brisk business would make the owner, Fred Wickshire, happy. I pulled into a spot next to Dax's SUV and turned off the engine. Lily had her hand on the door.

I touched her leg to stop her. "Do you want to tell me what's going on?

"Nothing."

I tipped my chin down and looked at her more intently. "Lily. The way you and Dax reacted and Milo chirping the way he did, something must be."

She stared out the windshield. We were looking in the direction of the gray clapboard building as if it suddenly captivated her attention. "The couple, Petra Addington and Simon were rude in the store, and it bothered me. And when she insisted they see the exhibit tonight, I became curious. Milo told me about the connection to a witch. I know how I would feel if my necklace were taken from me. I'm sure Dax had the same reaction."

"Is that really all there is to this situation?"

She nodded at the building. "We should go in. I'm starving, and Dax will think we took a detour." With that she pushed open the door and got out, effectively ending the conversation.

At least she waited for me in front of the truck. Although I didn't want to keep going over it in my head, I had the distinct impression there was more going on here. Who knows, maybe during dinner I could steer the conversation in the direction of the exhibit and get her and Dax talking. I hated being devious, but anything that caused the color to drain from my fiancé's face was worth getting to the bottom of as quickly as possible.

Lily looped her arm through the crook of mine and hummed as we walked inside. Fred greeted us with an expansive smile the minute he saw us. Clasping Lily's hand in his, he said, "Hello, you two. Dax is already inside." He picked up two menus from the host stand and said, "Follow me." Over his shoulder he grinned. "Have you given any more thought to your wedding reception? I would love to host it right here. We can shut the entire place down, and you can decorate it however you'd like. And I will guarantee you won't find a man dressed as a leprechaun dead in a bathroom."

I grimaced. "Thanks, Fred. We'll keep this place in mind." I thought it was a little too soon to be casually talking about the Pembroke Cove Bed & Breakfast incident and Nikki and Steve's wedding. But I was more surprised Lily hadn't reacted to his comment.

Fred set the menus down on a table that overlooked the saltwater marsh. The sun was beginning to set, casting deep orange, pink, and purple colors dancing on the surface of the water. It might be the perfect night for a romantic stroll on the beach after dinner.

Dax held up his pint glass of beer. "I ordered you each one, Lily the pale ale, and for you, Gage the stout."

Fred pulled out Lily's chair. "I will be right back with them. Specials are on the inside of the menu, and not to worry, I'll make sure extra rolls and butter come out too."

Lily smiled. "Fred, you're the best. Always remembering just how much I love your rolls."

He hurried away, waving to the waitress nearby, which I guessed meant rolls and beer would be delivered momentarily. "This was a great idea, Dax. Now that your news has settled, have you made a decision about the police chief job or are you still on the fence?"

He waited for half a minute as if gathering his thoughts. "There are two sides to this problem, and Lily, Gage, I'd like your honest opinion."

"Is there any other kind?" Lily asked.

One side of his mouth curled into a grin. "Not when it comes to you. But here's the issue. When I decided to take the job here, for the first time in years, I felt like I belonged. I have friends who have become family. A job I enjoy without the stress and bureaucracy of the DC gig." He tapped the top of the table and leaned forward. "But, to have the opportunity to lead a team, even if it's a small town with just four officers, I could make a real difference."

Our waitress came over as if she was being chased by a hurricane-force wind. She plopped down a bread basket overflowing with rolls and two pints of beer for me and Lily. Before we had the chance to say thank you, she said, "I'll be back in a jiffy for your orders."

Lily leaned closer to Dax. "What is it that's calling you to the job?"

"Do you remember the first time I went to Robins Pointe to investigate Archie Dane's death? As I drove down the charming main street, it reminded me of my hometown."

She blinked. "The one in Louisiana? Where the temperature is always above freezing, that hometown? And if I recall those days in December, the air was frigid. It was snowing every day. So how was it like home?"

Dax shook his head and chuckled. "Only you would compare the weather from one place to the other. I can't put it into words. It felt like I was slipping on my favorite sweatshirt, the one where its super soft from going through the washer a million times, and the tags are ripped out so it doesn't itch the back of your neck."

I knew exactly what he meant. After I moved away, all I could think about was when I could get back to Pembroke. It had taken a while longer for Lily to move home, but when she did, my life had fallen into place. "A while ago, you mentioned that you were looking or hoping to find someone special. Do you think that's another reason why you're being lulled to Robins Pointe? I don't want to have to rescue you from the depths of the Atlantic and a mermaid."

"No, it won't be with a mermaid, just a witch. And for the record, she's coming as fast as she can. I'd like to be ready to meet her when the time is right."

Lily sat up straight in her chair. "Then it's settled. Call the chairman of the town board tomorrow, and tell him you'll take the job, but you have to give notice here. I think you can start two weeks from Monday." She picked up her glass and glanced in the direction of my glass so I'd do the same. "Dax, I'd like to propose a toast. To your new adventure. But always remember you have people in Pembroke Cove who love you, so don't be a stranger."

We all tapped our glasses and drank to Lily's words.

"Tomorrow, stop at the store, and we'll start house hunting for you. We can even call Gretchen Wilson and see if she can help. I'm sure she shows property at the Pointe too."

"I'm not sure she'll want to help me since I was pretty convinced she had killed Teddy Roberts last year." Dax twirled his fork between his fingers.

Lily plopped her hand on top of it, stopping it mid-spin. "I thought she was guilty too, but she understands it's part of the investigation process. It's water under the bridge now."

Fred came over and gave us an apologetic smile. "Hey, sorry about the delay. We're busy tonight with that exhibit at the library, people are stopping in for dinner. It's great for business, but I hadn't planned to be fully staffed. What can I get you? The fried fish special has been getting rave reviews."

Lily said, "I'll have that with a cup of lobster bisque."

Dax and I both agreed that we'd have the same. Fred said it wouldn't be long and left us.

Dax said, "It's going to be fun checking out the new places to eat in Robins Pointe. You both will have to come help me eat my way through them all."

Dax, Lily, and I waddled out of the Clam Shack.

"Lily, I'll bring the coffee and pastry tomorrow as long as you're still willing to help me house hunt. I should buy a place and not rent, showing the townspeople I intend to stick around."

She stood on her tiptoes and kissed his cheek. "If you bring cinnamon pecan buns, I'll even help you pack your apartment."

"Deal." He said good night.

I slipped my arm around Lily's waist and kissed her. "How about a walk on the beach before I take you home. Maybe we can talk about our wedding reception, after all, I think this was like the tenth time Fred has offered up this place."

"That sounds like the perfect ending to our night." She took my hand. We strolled down the dock to where we could access the sandy beach. She slipped off her shoes and carried them in her hand, and I did the same. The tide was on its way out as the full moon hung in the sky, its glow providing just enough light as we strolled.

"Have you given any thought to when you'd like to make it official and marry me?" My heart skittered in my chest. We had gotten engaged at Halloween and had an engagement party at Christmas. So far, Lily hadn't been like any other bride I knew. She wanted us to take our time setting the date. If I could have, I would have married her the day after she said yes. I loved her, and she wanted us to enjoy taking things slow. After all, we had a lifetime to be married.

I heard her take a rapid breath.

"Gage." She tugged my hand urging me to move quicker. "Look." She pointed to the sandy strip of beach near an outcropping of rocks directly ahead of us. "Who's that?"

I dropped Lily's hand and ran the last few feet to where a body was lying face up in the wet sand. The outgoing tide lapped gently at her ankles. I knelt next to her. It was Petra Addington. Her eyes were wide and unseeing. I knew before I touched her wrist that she was dead.

Lily had activated her flashlight on her cell phone. "Oh, my stars. Petra?"

I held out my arms to keep Lily from getting to close as she waved the light down Petra's body.

"Gage, what's in her hand?" Lily's phone made a soft clicking sound as she took pictures.

I didn't have any gloves, and we needed to get pictures for evidence. I carefully leaned closer. "Well, this is something I wouldn't have expected."

I stretched out a hand, and she grabbed it back. "Don't touch anything. She's clutching the amulet."

Chapter 4
Lily

I couldn't believe what I was seeing. Petra was dead. However, the intriguing question was how the heck had she gotten the amulet from the library. "We need Dax to get over here right away."

Gage's lips thinned as he withdrew his cell. "Dax. I need you near the pier behind the restaurant. We have a body."

Then he was on the phone instructing Peabody and Mac to run by the library and see if anything looked out of place. "Dax is on his way here." He nodded a couple of times and said, "Let me know what you find."

I was glad Gage had listened to me. He needed a witch of Dax's caliber to cast a protection spell against whatever was going on with that amulet. I wouldn't betray Milo's secret, but I'd figure out what I could say to convince Dax that extra care needed to be taken at this crime scene.

Gage sat on a rock and brushed off his feet. He glanced at my pink polished toenails. "We should put our shoes on in case there is something in the sand, like a needle. Based on the yellow in her eyes and the pallor of her skin, my first guess is poison. How it was administered won't be apparent until the EL gets her on his table. With any luck, the autopsy will be able to pinpoint exactly what happened to her."

I had my doubts the town's medical examiner could detect a curse, but that wasn't something I needed to worry about. He was excellent at his job. The sounds of sirens drew closer. Above the sand dunes, doors slamming meant we were about to get a lot of company. It was several minutes before we saw Dax or the other police officers. They must have taken a few moments to unload some large portable floodlights, which now lit up the jetty and poor Petra like high noon in June.

Dax slogged through the sand, a grimace was plastered on his face. I smothered a small smile. I guessed he wasn't a fan of getting sand in his shoes.

"What have we got here?" He knelt down next to the body and snapped on latex gloves.

Before he could touch her, I yanked on his shirt sleeve. "Dax. Wait."

He glanced at his shirt clutched in my fingers. "Lily, do you know something?"

There were people swarming around the scene, and I couldn't take the risk of being overheard. I took a few steps closer to the water and he followed me. The waves would muffle our conversation. Gage was busy talking to another officer and didn't pay any mind as we stepped away.

"There's something you should know, about the amulet."

His eyebrow arched, but he didn't ask questions. He

had assumed Gage's way of questioning people and that was to wait until they started babbling. Not that I needed to play this game of cat and mouse. I inwardly groaned when I thought of Milo.

"Here's the thing. Milo gave me the history of the red opal. At one time, it was imbued with goodness until someone tried to steal it. Then the witch, who it had been stolen from, cursed it. Whoever wore the amulet would die. With Petra clutching it, the curse must have gotten to her. I need for you to cast a strong protection spell. The curse must be contained in a protective bubble so no one else gets hurt." I grasped his hand. "Please Dax, can you do this and not tell Gage."

He glanced over his shoulder and saw police officers were taking pictures of the scene. "Is that why Peabody and Mac aren't here, you need backup and for me to perform magic on a crime scene?"

"Yes, I'm not accomplished enough to be certain my spell would be strong enough."

"I don't like tampering with a crime scene, but this is a special circumstance." He gave a brisk nod. "We'll use this as a teaching moment." He looked around and flashed me a wink, "First, there's too much going on to cast a decent spell. We'll change that."

He faced the ocean, his arms at his sides but palms open, facing the water. "From sea to land for I command, freeze the crime scene I demand. For this, I wish so mote it be."

When I looked at where Gage had been talking to one of the EMTs, it was as if he was flash-frozen. Like in a cartoon except there wasn't an icicle dangling from his nose. "Wow, how did you do that?"

He grinned. "It's one of the spells I perfected when I was on the job in DC. Investigators are overworked and move at the speed of light. There were times when important clues got overlooked. This way I could take a few minutes, poke around, unfreeze everyone, and then point out the clue. It was useful but not something I abused."

He strode over the sand and stopped when he was beside our victim. He pulled a small flashlight from his pocket and trained it over her right hand. "I see the chain, but are you sure it's the amulet from the exhibit?"

I nodded. How could I explain the connection Milo had and now me? It was like it was calling to me to reach out and rescue it and return it to the rightful owner, my familiar. "Look closer. The colors are unmistakable."

He walked around her body and stopped at her feet. "Did you notice she's still wearing high heels?"

"Why didn't she take them off before coming down here?"

Dax shot me a grim look. "She might not have come here under her own steam. She could have been carried and left after she was already dead."

I withdrew my phone and snapped a bunch more pictures. Dax knew my mind was in hyperdrive, and the lure of getting involved in another murder would be too much for me to resist. What he didn't know is I had a slight advantage understanding the real history of the curse.

When I stuffed the phone back in my pocket, he said, "I was serious before that this would be a teaching opportunity. Are you ready to help me? The power of two witches is better than one. I could use a third since what we're trying to do is contain something that is not meant to be."

"I'll help. How can you protect EL when he starts to do the autopsy?"

"What we're about to cast will protect all the non-magicals who come in contact with Petra. And that will include people like Gage who were born of a witch. We can't take the chance that anyone else will be hurt by this curse if, in fact, it's real."

"Oh, the curse is real."

He gave me another razor-sharp look. "Lily, I need for you to be totally honest with me. Tell me everything you know."

I longed to unburden myself; he might be able to help. But I would never betray Milo's secret to anyone. Our bond had to be one hundred percent pure. "I'm sorry Dax, I've told you everything I can."

He gave me a long, assessing look. "All right, you know I'm here if you need to talk." He held out his hand, and I took it. His warmth soothed my jangled nerves. "Ready to do this?"

"Yes, what do you need me to do first?"

"We're going to stand on each side of her and our joined hands will be across her body. As I speak the words, I want you to close your eyes and repeat them after me. Don't let go of my hands until I finish. I'll give you a squeeze when I'm done."

My stomach clenched in a knot. I swallowed hard. "Will something bad happen if I do?"

His smile reassured me that I was freaking out for no reason. "It just increases our magic to be connected."

He moved next to Petra's right hand where the amulet rested. Extending his arms, I mirrored him and took his hands.

"Close your eyes."

I did, and Dax began to speak in slow, clear words.

"For protection from evil, for protection from a witch's curse."

I repeated the same words with the same intensity that Dax had.

"We request protection for all mortals who may not understand the power that rests in this woman's hand."

Again, I said the words exactly as Dax did. The wind kicked up around us.

"We plead our case for protection for all, as we wish so it shall be."

When we said the final statement one last time I opened my eyes and met Dax's. He gave a half nod of approval. "You have the power of three." He applied slight pressure to my fingers and released my hands. He then said, "Return the scene to as it once was, for this I wish so it shall be."

Conversations picked up right where they left off. Gage looked at me and Dax, and his brow creased. We were standing over Petra, which we hadn't been before Dax cast the first spell. Gage scratched his cheek as if trying to puzzle together what had happened. It was something I'd fill him in on later.

Now that the scene was safe, I walked a short distance to give the professionals room to do their job. If Petra was here, where was Simon? I walked down the beach and called the Coastal Motel. My hunch was they were staying there. Easy access to town and the library. If Petra had been intent on stealing the amulet, she would be less conspicuous at the motel.

Torrie, the front desk attendant answered, "Coastal Motel. Torrie speaking."

"Hi Torrie, it's Lily."

"Hey there, what's going on?"

I hadn't spoken to her since the magicians had rolled through town a few weeks ago. Sadly, this time, the conversation might sound redundant. "Hi, Torrie. I had a couple of customers in the shop today, Petra Addington and Simon, I'm not sure of his last name. Are they staying at the motel?"

"Yes, I have a reservation for them, but Ms. Addington and Mr. Beale haven't checked in yet. They're planning on staying two nights. Can I give them a message when they check in?"

"That would be great. They were looking for some books, and I have one that they might find interesting. Please let Petra know she can stop by tomorrow after ten. I've put it aside for her."

A pang of guilt pierced my heart since I knew Petra would never get the message.

"Will do. And any chance you could pre-order that new release by Maddie James, the cozy mystery set in Harbor Falls. Advance buzz tells me it's going to be a good addition to her series."

"Sure thing, Torrie. I'll check the release date and let you know when I'll get it in the store."

"Thanks, Lily. Not to worry, if Ms. Addington doesn't check in soon, I'll leave a note on the office door."

"I appreciate that. Have a good night."

"What did you find out?" Gage's voice caused me to jump.

I spun around. "Sorry. I thought you were busy back there." I looked over his shoulder as the EMTs lifted Petra from the sand. Waiting until she was secured to the gurney and the sheet covered her, I said, "She and her friend Simon Beale are scheduled to check into the Coastal Motel and stay two nights. But Torrie said they haven't arrived yet. So, either he just hasn't gotten around to it, changed his mind, they were planning to stay someplace else, or something bad has happened to Simon, too."

"Try not to borrow trouble when it comes to Simon Beale. I have a funny feeling he'll show up sooner or later." His gaze trailed to where mine was locked. "Thanks for connecting with the motel. I'll call Peabody and ask her to check out the B & B for Mr. Beale. He needs to tell us about his friend."

"I don't think they're friends, but they work together. By the way she was treating him, my guess is he's her assistant." I snapped my fingers. "Shoot, I should have asked Torrie about the three people who were arguing with Petra at the library."

"Lily, please let me do my job. I'll follow up with Torrie regarding Roni, Donella, and Chaz. With a little bit of luck, they're staying either there or the B & B, and I can get their last names too."

I pulled out my phone. "I'll call Torrie, it will only take a couple of minutes, and you can get back to doing your job." I jabbed my finger in Dax's direction. He was waving his hand at us. "It looks like he needs to talk to you."

Gage took my phone and slipped it into his shirt pocket and then pecked my cheek. "I'll give this back to you when we're in the truck."

I crossed my arms over my midsection and gave him my best frown. "It's not like I was going to go and track them down. It was just a phone call."

With a small shake of his head, he said, "And one myself or the officers can make."

I stood up straighter. "Maybe I should take the truck and see if Sharon and Mac are still at the library. I'd like to see how she got into the annex."

"Lily."

There was no mistaking the warning tone in his voice. I held up my hands as if I was surrendering. "I know. Stay out of it. But just so that you're fully aware, I will be setting up my clue board as soon as I get home. This is too good of a mystery to not examine the clues."

"What clues?"

"A dead woman, wearing high heels on the beach, clutching a cursed amulet in her hand, and her companion's nowhere to be found." I had to contain my grin out of respect for the victim. "You have to admit this is something that stirs my cauldron."

He shook his head. "You can make notes on your board. But don't start asking questions to my growing suspect list. Every time you do, you find danger. At this point, I have four good suspects. They were all at the exhibit and, based on the argument we witnessed, have a motive to want to keep Petra away from the amulet."

A finger of fear slid down my spine as he headed in Dax's direction. If being at the library was a reason to be a suspect, should Milo be on the list? After all, he was the original owner of the priceless and powerful necklace. I shook off the fear that moved from my spine and wrapped around my heart and soul. Above all else, I would protect Milo even if I had to pry answers out of him after some very difficult questions. The first was whether Petra Addington was killed by his curse. I was afraid of the answer. Could he be responsible?

Chapter 5
Lily

Gage opened the kitchen door. I kicked off my sand-filled shoes just outside on the deck. It was late, and I was surprised Milo hadn't greeted us. "Milo. We're home."

He didn't slink around the door casing. I glanced at Gage and said, "Let me check on him." I went into each room but couldn't find him. My heart rate kicked up, and my breathing followed.

Once I was back in the kitchen, Gage asked, "What's wrong?"

"Milo's missing?"

"Sweetheart. I'm sure he's fine. You know, out doing his familiar get-together thing. You said he does that from time to time."

I looked at the kitty door and took several deep breaths. I couldn't appear irrational about Milo not being home. It might make Gage ask questions that I wanted to avoid. "You're right. Do you want to have tea before you head home?"

He wrapped his arms around me and nuzzled my neck. "I would like nothing more, but poor Brutus was expecting me hours ago, and I'm sure he needs to go outside."

I hugged him tight. "I'm glad you rescued him. It's good you're not going home to an empty house."

"My mom always had a cat as her familiar. I never thought I was a dog person, let alone a Great Dane. But, the truth is, and don't tell Nikki since this was her idea for me to take the big lug, Brutus rescued me. The bonus is my dog and your familiar get along beautifully."

"They do. Well, it's been a long day. You should go and take care of him. Text me when you get home." I pulled open the kitchen door and bussed Gage on the lips. Hopefully, he didn't feel like I was pushing him out the door, but I couldn't shake the fear that was suffocating my heart. Something was terribly wrong with Milo.

"Okay." With a slow, simmering kiss we said goodnight and he promised to text when he got home.

I waited until he had backed out of the driveway before I crossed to the end of the deck. I lifted my face to the stars and said, "Two peas in a pod are we. I need to see what Milo can see. This spell is not to be used frivolously. This I wish, and so it shall be."

Inky darkness was in front of me. Was Milo sleeping? I took several deep, slow breaths. A witch in a state of panic was ineffective for spell casting. "Find my familiar for me, so this I wish, so it shall be."

It was as if I was zooming out on an image. Milo was lying under a bush in front of the library's stone steps, unmoving. I raced into the house and grabbed my car keys. During the drive, I told myself over and over again that he was napping and I was being foolish. I reached the parking lot in record time, threw my car in park, and raced to where he lay, calling to him as I fell to my knees.

I extended my fingers, unsure if touching him would cause him pain. Tentatively, I stroked his soft, gray fur. His body was warm to the touch and relief washed over me. He was alive. "Milo, come on big boy. Wake up." He didn't open his eyes or lift his head. His sides moved up and down with each deep, labored breath he took. I closed my eyes slipped my hands under his limp body, and cradled him close to me. I said, "Come on, little man, we're going to go see Aunt Mimi."

By the time I got to my aunt's house, I had run through every possible scenario. Had he been attacked by another animal? He didn't have any wounds, and he wasn't bleeding. Was it his heart? Or had Milo been cursed? Cold, icy fingers wrapped around my throat. That was the only thing that made sense. My next biggest worry was whether he would be okay. As I pulled up to the front door, the outside light clicked on, illuminating the driveway. Aunt Mimi was standing in the doorway with her husband Nate next to her. I reminded myself to keep it together. I needed to be strong.

Nate hurried to the car and opened the passenger door. I put my hand out. "I've got him."

He gave a respectful nod and watched as I picked Milo up. He took my elbow as he guided me up the walk. Aunt Mimi opened the door wider and ushered me inside.

"Lily, what happened?"

I didn't bother to ask how she knew I was coming. Our connection seemed to have few limitations. "When I got home from the crime scene, the house was empty. At first, I thought it was no big deal. However, I had this feeling something was wrong. As if the world wasn't spinning correctly. I cast a spell to see what Milo could see, there was impenetrable blackness around me. Then I cast another spell and discovered he was under a bush near the entrance to the library."

She arched a brow and steered me into the kitchen. "What crime scene?" She gestured to the blanket-covered table. I carefully placed Milo down in the middle with my hand still resting on him so I could feel his sides rise and fall.

"It's a long story, but my only concern is for Milo." I felt the tears prick my eyes, and with the back of my hand, swept them away. There would be time enough for tears of relief once I knew he was going to be fine.

Phoenix, my aunt's familiar, jumped onto the table and walked around him as she sniffed Milo's fur. "Mimi, you must hurry. There's a poison overtaking his body."

"How much time do we have?"

I heard the urgency in Phoenix's sweet kitty voice. It yanked at my heart strings. If Phoenix was worried, then my fear wasn't misplaced.

"An hour, maybe less."

"What kind of poison are we dealing with?" Mimi opened a cabinet where she stored medicinal herbs and potions.

Once again, Phoenix walked around Milo pausing to sniff every inch of his soft, downy fur. How I wished he would open his eyes and tell me to read the book or call me his dear witch.

"I'm not sure, but it's on his face. We need to start by washing it off. Then, you can brew an antidote; it will need to be strong. Without the exact component, go broad. Nothing you will do can make the situation worse."

"I'll bathe him. Whatever is on his fur is already on me since I've held him in my arms."

Aunt Mimi looked at Nate, her face grim. "Run upstairs and get me a change of clothes for Lily." She peered into my face. "So far, you're unaffected, but there's no sense in taking any chances."

Now that she mentioned it, my protection necklace was very warm against my skin. Could it be that was working on overdrive to keep me safe from whatever Milo had come in contact with? Right now, Milo needed to be cleansed and then receive a potion. "What about you and Phoenix? I don't want anything happening to you either."

"When I knew you were coming I wrapped a protection spell around the house and enhanced it for Nate, Phoenix, and me." She cupped my cheek. "Believe in me and our magic."

Nate came back into the room and held out a tee shirt and fleece pants. Before I could take them, Mimi grabbed them and said, "Go into the bathroom and take a quick shower and put these on. By the time you come out, the water will be ready for Milo."

I did as I was told, completely trusting Aunt Mimi would do her best to save Milo. Phoenix continued to hover but didn't touch her old friend, and Nate waited to be of assistance to Mimi. We were all working toward the same goal.

As fast as I could, I dressed and came back into the kitchen. My towel-dried hair dripped water onto the tile floor. There was a basin at one end of the table, and Milo was in the same spot I left him. His side had a gentle movement with each inhale and slow exhale. At least it was a steady rhythm.

"What do I do now, Aunt Mimi." I tucked my pendant inside my tee shirt.

"First, come here." She pointed to her side. "I'll cast a new protection spell around you. It will increase the power of your amulet. Then, I want you to start with Milo's face and head. Wash them with the bar of soap next to the tub, and cleanse each area three times. Then move to his chest and front legs, down his back and belly, and finish with his hind legs and tail. Towel him dry. Once that is over, wrap him in the green wool blanket that is warming next to the wood stove. You'll cradle him in your arms while I administer the potion."

I noticed a stack of towels, all shades of green and the emerald green blanket on top. "Why green?"

"It's for health and vitality." She stepped to where her cauldron was beginning to steam and dropped ingredients in it, the entire time speaking a soft incantation.

I didn't need to hear the words to know we were moving in the right direction. "I'm sorry sweet boy. You hate baths, but this is the most important one of your life."

Doing as my aunt instructed I washed Milo exactly the way she had said. The water was changing each time I started a new round. It ranged from clear to a milky gray, and by the third time it was black.

"Aunt Mimi, should I wash him again. The water is disgusting."

She looked over my shoulder. "That won't be necessary. You did a fine job."

I gave Milo a good rub down with a warm towel. Then I took the blanket and swaddled him like a baby. I got as close to the wood stove as I dared and crooned softly to him. My throat was thick, and I could barely say, "Stay with me, Milo." I rubbed between his ears. Tears slipped down my cheeks. "I need you to teach me everything that I've missed, being a late bloomer and all."

My aunt gestured for me to sit down. She knelt in front of me. Using an eyedropper, she began to slip one tiny drop at a time in his little mouth. "Keep urging him to fight."

"Milo, did you hear Aunt Mimi? She said you need to fight your way back to me. Come on, you know you can't leave me to fumble through learning spells without you."

She slipped more into his mouth. Phoenix was now perched on the small side table next to my chair.

This process continued for the next fifteen minutes until the dropper was empty. Aunt Mimi sat back on her heels. "Phoenix, what do you think?"

"It's working, but this will take more time. I can feel him fighting to come back."

The blanket was damp from my tears. I wasn't going to have to say goodbye, at least not today. "Come on, old man. Open your eyes. I've got that salmon you like at home."

I changed out the blanket for a dry green towel. I

rubbed his paws between the velour fabric and said, "I need you, Milo. Please open your eyes."

I stared intently at his little face. His nose twitched. "Milo, come on baby. Open your eyes for your favorite witch." The minutes dragged on.

Finally it seemed he was struggling to open his eyes. "Aunt Mimi. Look."

Phoenix tapped him on the head. "Old man, open your eyes."

They fluttered open, and then closed again. But he squirmed in my arms. "Come on, Milo."

"My. Dear. Witch." Each word was barely audible but he spoke.

I crushed him to my chest and began to sob happy tears. "Milo, you are going to be fine."

Aunt Mimi was still kneeling in front of me, and she rubbed my knee "Lily, let him breathe." There was a lightness to her words as she spoke.

Milo opened his eyes and stared into mine. "Don't cry, my little witch." His gaze darted around the room, and I could feel his heart rate quicken. "I'm confused. What happened, and how did we get here?"

"I was hoping you could tell me. I found you at the library, and Phoenix said you were poisoned. What do you remember?"

He struggled to a sitting position, and I kept my hand under his tummy while my fingers ran the length of his body, reassuring me and keeping our connection strong.

"After you and Gage left for dinner, I went to the library. I wanted to stand guard over the you know what." He gave me a side eye as if reminding me to stay silent.

"Those awful people snuck into the library through a side door. Which reminds me, you need to tell Paige to make sure all doors are locked before she leaves."

Milo was definitely feeling more like himself. "Go on."

He dropped his head. "That's just it, all I can remember is seeing them and waiting." He gave me a long, assessing look. "You came looking for me. Why? What happened?"

"Petra Addington was found tonight on the beach near the Clam Shack. She's dead, and she was holding the Heart of the Soul amulet in her right hand."

Aunt Mimi looked from me to Milo, and Phoenix leaned in closer to us.

My aunt asked, "Are you talking about the red opal that was cursed by a witch?"

Nodding, I swallowed hard. I wasn't sure what to say or not. I gently poked Milo's back side, hoping he'd get the hint to say something. When he didn't, I decided the basic information was my only option.

"There's a traveling exhibit of amulets and some other artifacts like old pottery, hand carved buttons, and even some small paintings on what appear to be roof tiles. It opened earlier yesterday and is scheduled to be at the library for two weeks before it moves on to the next town."

"And this opal was a part of the collection?" my aunt asked.

"Yes, it's beautiful. Whatever metal was used was woven around the stone, and the colors seemed to bounce from the light. I've never seen a necklace with such workmanship." Milo pressed his claws into my leg, and it brought me back to this conversation. "Sorry, I got carried away. When I heard that this particular piece was part of the exhibit, I went with Milo, Gage, and Dax to check it out. This nasty woman, who had been in the bookshop earlier today started arguing with these other three people, and it just got downright ugly. Arguing about who was going to get the opportunity to examine it. Finally, all five of them left. But I got the distinct impression the argument would continue."

"Five? You only mentioned four." Mimi said, "This Petra woman and the three others that seemed to be frenemies."

"Petra had a man with her. Simon Beale," I said. "Milo, if what you remember is true, Petra must have decided to steal the necklace. Something went horribly wrong, and the curse killed her."

Mimi eased back into a chair. "I have something to add. When I was a young witch, I had the opportunity to see that particular amulet up close and personal, and when I did, I held it. The curse must have faded over time since as you can see I'm still alive and well."

Milo rose to his feet and his fur spiked down the length of his spine. "That's not possible. The witch who cast the spell was extremely powerful."

"Yes, but..." she held up her index finger before Milo or I could interrupt her. "The spell that was cast was against witches who wanted to use it to do harm. And it could never hurt a non-magical."

"Why would you think that?" Milo grumbled.

"I am a powerful witch, and back in the day, I was charged with investigating centuries-old artifacts to determine if, in fact they could cause harm. It was then I discovered the twist on the legend. Rest assured, the amulet didn't kill that woman. Now it will be up to the police to determine what did, and unless I lost my touch, Milo came in contact with a poison on a much smaller scale."

"Your protection spell must have been working overtime." Milo grumbled, "Or you, too, would have fallen victim to the amulet of Aathmika."

I gave an involuntary shudder hoping Aunt Mimi would overlook that Milo had used the original name for the amulet. "Are you saying Milo could have died tonight?"

He patted my cheek with his paw. "Don't worry, Lily. I'm not going anywhere. After all, as a cat, I have nine lives, and as of tonight I have eight left."

"I'm not sure I have that many, so let's not do this again, please." I kissed Milo on the top of his head. "What do you say we go home."

Chapter 6
Gage

The following morning, with a spring in my step, I crossed the town square. My destination was to see Lily. When I grew closer to the bookstore, I noticed Milo through the window. He was sleeping on the cushion in the front window, and Lily was at the counter reading. Dax had said he would bring coffee and muffins, so I was going to swoop in and steal a few moments with my girl.

I pushed open the door, and she looked up. A smile graced her lush lips. "Hey, stranger." She looked around. "Where's Dax? He promised coffee."

"He'll be here soon, but I wanted a few minutes alone with you." I pulled her to her feet and wrapped my arms around her waist. "Our romantic stroll on the beach was interrupted."

"It was." She looked at the book she had set aside.

"What are you reading?"

"Nothing. Just doing a little research."

That hitch in the tone of her voice said there was more

to it than casual interest. I released her and stepped closer to the counter and picked up the book. "Rare Plants of the Northeast." I leafed through the pages and noted she had earmarked several pages with post-it notes. The last page she had marked was Devil's Hemlock. I scanned the page, and it was a poison that could prove to be fatal just by inhaling it. "Lily, why are you looking up this information? Do you think the victim was poisoned with something in this book?"

She glanced at Milo, who was now wide awake and sitting up. He began to meow softly at first, and as Lily shook her head, he got louder. Slapping her hands against her legs, she said, "Fine. I'll tell him. But he's going to have a lot of questions."

Milo dipped his head and turned his back to her.

"Will you please tell me what that was all about?" I thrust the book to her, "And does this have anything to do with it?"

Lily took the book from my hand and placed it on the counter. She steered me to the wingback chairs. "Have a seat."

The hairs on the back of my neck stood at attention. I licked my lips and waited for her to get settled. Patience was the key here just like when I was questioning a suspect. Not that I was about to question my fiancé but alarm bells were starting to sound in my head.

"Do you remember last night how Milo wasn't home when we got there?"

She took my hand, and I kept my eyes locked on hers. Her pupils were wide, her face pale. "You thought he had gone out carousing like usual."

Her gaze darted to Milo and then back to me. "I cast a spell so I could see what he was seeing. I figured if he was hanging out with other familiars I could go to bed and not worry. When I did, all I saw was black. It scared me. I didn't want to invade his privacy, but I had a sinking feeling something was wrong. I cast another spell to help me find him. At this point, I was sure he was unable to connect with me."

"He was hurt?"

"Worse." The word came out in a stutter, and her body shuddered. "He was lying on the ground near the library. I couldn't get there fast enough. Thank the stars I wasn't too late, but it was touch and go. From there, I raced him to Aunt Mimi. Between her and Phoenix, they saved him. Some poison had gotten on his fur, and he doesn't know how it happened."

"Sweetheart, why didn't you call me right away? I would have come."

Lily shook her head. "You had a job to do, but Gage, I think what happened to Milo is connected to Petra's death." She squeezed my hand. "Before you say I'm taking a giant leap, hear me out."

"Before you continue..." I crossed the room to the window seat and gently picked up Milo. Holding him close to my chest I said, "Hi, old man, I'm glad you're okay."

He looked up at me, his eyes wide and glassy. It was as if he had a hangover. He meowed at me, and Lily laughed softly.

"He said, *watch who you're calling old.*"

"I'm sorry, Milo; I didn't mean to offend you." I placed

him in her arms. "Now you can tell me how you believe these two incidents are connected."

Milo turned around on her lap and finally settled in; with his eyes closed, he began to snore softly. Lily ran her hand from the top of his head down his back. It made me wonder who it was soothing more, witch or familiar?

"Milo was out doing his usual stroll when he witnessed Petra, Simon, and the other three from the exhibit enter the library via a side door. As they entered, he heard them talking about stealing the amulet, and he was waiting to see what happened next. Being from the witch community, he understands the power of the necklace. He knew if it fell into a non-magical person's hands, it would be like someone unleashing an evil genie from a bottle."

"Why didn't he just find a way to contact you, and, in turn, you could tell me there had been a break-in at the exhibit?"

"He was taking the wait-and-see approach. To be honest, I would have done the same thing. Like would they be successful in actually committing the crime?" She narrowed her eyes. "Why didn't the alarm go off? We know Petra was successful since she was clutching the amulet in her hand when she was found."

I felt the frown crease my forehead. "When I scanned Mac's report, it didn't mention a break-in at the library last night." I withdrew my phone and texted Mac. I hated to question my officers, but this was more important. Milo had been somehow caught in the crossfire of whatever happened there last night.

Are you sure the library was secured last night? Check

inside and get back to me. I need to know if anything is out of place.

The response was immediate. I read it out loud, "Alright, Mac said the library was locked up and there was no visual indication anyone had been inside. Since all looked normal they didn't go in. He and Peabody are on their way, and he'll let me know what they find soon." I put my cell in my jeans pocket.

She continued to pet Milo. "The side door was open. Why did Paige leave it unlocked? Was she assisting them in the crime?"

I knew where she was going and said, "Hold that thought." I walked into the back room and glanced around the tidy space. A small blackboard was leaning against the wall. Lily had an identical board at home to keep track of clues in a case. From past experience, both of these boards were about to be put into action.

Lily smiled as I returned with the board and set it up so that she could see it, but it was directly visible from the street. If a customer came into the store she could make it appear blank with a flick of her wrist. I was proud of how accomplished she had become in such a short time.

"Thank you for reading my mind."

I picked up the chalk. "What time did Milo say he saw the archeologists enter the library?"

She twisted her mouth to one side and looked down at the sleeping cat. "That's right. Petra mentioned her status as a doctor during her argument with the newcomers."

Nodding, I wrote down Petra Addington at the top of the board. I listed in a column on the left Simon Beale,

Roni Blake, Donella Hoffman, and Chaz Tate, and, as an afterthought, added Paige Reed.

"Add amulet next to Petra's name and the time we found her. I'm going to guess that the medical examiner hasn't called yet with any details."

"EL said he should know something by mid-morning." I jotted, 9:00 PM, to the left of Petra's name. "I took you home around ten. What time did you go to the library, and besides finding Milo, did you see anything out of the ordinary?"

She looked out the window watching but not seeing what was going on. I knew her thoughts were on rewind as she replayed the scene in her head. "I found Milo around ten fifteen. Everything was dark except for the normal lights. I didn't see any people either. Of course, when I discovered Milo he was my sole focus."

"Do you think he'll wake up and fill us in on a few details?" Before she could answer, my cell phone chirped with an incoming message. "It's from Mac. There is no sign of a break-in, but the case that held the Heart of the Soul amulet has been cut open, and that is the only item missing."

With a shake of her head, she looked at the floor. "Gage, Of course it was. We saw it in Petra's hand, and it was the only object they were arguing about. The rest of the display was inconsequential to them."

I didn't say I had hoped we had been mistaken about what she was holding since I wasn't an expert in amulets. "Let's get back to where we started. Milo. Do you think someone deliberately wanted to harm him and if yes, why? To a non-magical he's a cat."

"I'm going out on a broom here and say it was an accident. He was in the wrong place at the wrong time, and something got on his fur. As he sat there watching, he must have breathed the poison in and then collapsed." She looked at me as tears filled her eyes and she choked back a sob. "I was almost too late."

I dropped to a knee and wrapped my arms around her and Milo. Kissing her cheek, I said, "But you weren't. He's here, and he will be fine. Your aunt Mimi is a great healer."

Tears rolled unchecked down her cheeks and dropped to Milo. He lifted his head and purred. My heart felt as if it would burst with the multitude of emotions that were building in me. I didn't want to think that someone would intentionally harm Milo. But, it was a possibility and not one I was about to say out loud.

The bell over the door jingled. Dax strode in juggling a cardboard tray of coffee and a bag of goodies. His brow arched when he caught my eye. "What's going on in here?"

Lily pulled from my arms. "Hi, Dax." She wiped her cheeks with the back of her hand. "I'm having a bit of a rough start."

"Are you upset you discovered another crime?"

I appreciated that he didn't say dead body. Not that Lily would shy away from the phrase, but putting dead into the conversation might remind her of what had almost happened to Milo. Which we still needed to get to the bottom of, and for that, I had to ask questions. Now that Dax was here and he spoke familiar we might be able to make progress.

He glanced at the clue board. "I see the puzzle sleuth is at work." He dragged a chair up to sit next to Lily and set the bag and tray on the small table between them. Milo lifted his head and Dax rubbed his ears. "What have I missed?"

I took the coffee cup he handed to me after he had given one to Lily. "We were just about to wake Milo and ask him what happened last night. It seems, somehow, his fur was doused with a poison that almost claimed his life."

"What?" His southern accent drawled out that one word with great force. "Is he going to be all right?"

Lily nodded. "It took a bit, but Aunt Mimi was able to get rid of it all, and after some rest, he'll be back to his normal self." Milo rolled over on his back and Lily rubbed his belly. "Are you ready to answer a few questions little man?"

He opened one eye and then the other before covering them with a paw. He meowed several times.

Dax grinned and Lily exhaled with a smile.

"And I'm sure that was some kind of comment about me?"

I waited as Dax gave Lily a wink, and he said, "Milo will tell his story, and he won't miss any detail too small, so no need for an interrogation from Pembroke Cove's ace detective. Which, to be honest, I thought I was the ace."

I was glad Dax had shown up. It added some lightness to the situation. Milo liked Dax and respected him, and it would help Lily in retelling Milo's account of what happened last night. I held up my hand and said, "I promise, no interrogation tactics will be used in conjunction with this conversation between two witches, a familiar and me."

Milo rose to a seated position and began to meow. Dax

leaned closer as if he was completely captivated by what was being said. As much as I wished I could hear first-hand what Milo was saying, Lily and Dax would fill in the story for me.

Dax asked, "That is the last thing you remember?"

Milo dipped his head and stretched out on Lily's lap while he stared at me. "Pick up where you left off before, about Milo taking the wait-and-see approach. How long did he sit there, and did he see anyone come out of the library?"

"He said after about a half hour they all came out, arguing like they had been earlier in the day, but he didn't see the amulet in anyone's hands, and he got the distinct impression they hadn't been successful. It was then Petra stopped. They were right in front of Milo. She demanded to know why they were all against her, even her assistant Simon. He had glanced at the building and heard Petra call someone an idiot, and she ran across the square. That is the last thing he remembers other than not feeling well."

"Who was she referring to as the idiot?"

Milo didn't need words to answer that question; the tip of his head and the grumble that came from deep in his chest were enough to tell me if he knew, he would have said the name. "Sorry Milo, but I had to ask."

Lily scooped him into her arms and stood up. "Milo says we need to head over to the library and survey the scene." She looked from Dax to me with an arched brow. "As my grandfather used to say, if we go now we won't need to hurry later. Are you coming?"

I wasn't about to remind her it was a crime scene. She had snuck into the library once before, and I'm sure she and

Milo would do it again. I held out my arms. "I'll carry Milo."

He snapped his head around and glared at me.

"What did I say wrong this time? I'm being the good guy here. You went through a lot last night."

He meowed, and Lily said, "Milo appreciates your concern, but he will walk. He said it wouldn't look good as a member of the familiar network to be carried through the town square."

I shook my head. There were some things I would never understand when it came to the magical part of our community.

Chapter 7
Lily

Milo and I waited while Gage lifted the crime scene tape from the door and I slipped in under it. Dax followed with Gage bringing up the rear. Of course, Milo trotted through the doorway, leading the way. I hurried after him, and he wove in and around tables, down aisles of books in the direction of the annex. The library was silent, like a tomb. Gage was now on my right and Dax was to my left.

Slowing my steps, I glanced at Gage. "Has anyone informed Paige of the robbery?"

"She's at the station answering questions with Mac and Peabody."

The door to the exhibit was closed, and I looked at Dax. "Do you sense any magical residue?" From what I had recently learned, when magic was performed, it could leave behind almost like a signature from the witch. I wasn't savvy enough to pick up on it, but this was a good learning opportunity.

Dax closed his eyes before saying. "No. I don't sense anything."

Milo wove himself around my legs. "My dear witch, there is one thing I can tell you with absolute certainty. Those people are not part of the magical community. If they were, they would not have wanted any part of my amulet."

Dax's eyebrows shot to his hairline. "What exactly do you mean Milo?"

I cringed. A slip of the tongue and Milo had divulged part of his secret. "You know how Milo is about all things witch. He thinks of everything in terms of his. Like my book, *Practical Beginnings*. He'll often refer to it as his too. And I'm his witch." I hoped it didn't sound like I was babbling even though I was.

"What did Milo say?" Gage looked from me to Dax and back to me again. "Lily, am I missing something that is critical to this case?"

"All Milo said was Petra and the others, who were here yesterday, couldn't be magical or they wouldn't have wanted the amulet with the curse and all." I snuck a look at Dax and couldn't help but notice the deep frown on his face. His eyes had narrowed and questions lingered there.

Since Dax didn't contradict my statement, which was mostly accurate, I relaxed. Gage pulled open the door. "Fine. No wandering off, we stick together and that includes Milo."

"He's no fun," Milo grumbled. I secretly agreed. Sticking together meant I couldn't look at the crime scene objectively. Instead, I'd have to block out Gage and Dax's commentary.

"Lights on," I said, and the room was awash with bright lights. There would be nothing hidden.

Dax nodded his approval. "Straight to the point, well done."

I stood a little straighter with his compliment, and Milo pawed my leg. "Don't get too excited. We have a crime to solve, and we must get the amulet back where it belongs before anyone else gets hurt."

"It's okay Milo. Dax cast a protection spell around it last night when we discovered Petra was clutching it in her hand."

He began to strut down the aisle when he stopped and slowly turned. "Did you say she was holding it?"

"Yes, it was in her right hand. Why?"

"When I, er, I mean when it was cursed, it was specific to wearing it, not just holding it." He started to head to the display case, which left me wondering if that was true, then how did Petra die?

"Gage, any news from EL yet?"

He pulled out his phone. "I'm sure he would have called." With a glance at the screen, he shook his head. "Nope."

Dax and Milo were standing in front of the now-empty case. Small pieces of what I thought were glass littered the floor. "Be careful Milo." I didn't want his paws to get cut.

"I'm fine." He tipped his head my way. "It's not real glass, some type of plastic, and it won't cause any injury."

Gage and I reached the cabinet, and the case was definitely empty. On the floor inside was a round clear disc from the case. "Was this the only artifact that was taken?" I couldn't pull my eyes from the empty space.

"According to Peabody, everything else is untouched."

I moved around Dax's other side and looked at the case from another angle. "This might sound stupid but I was hoping it was a bigger heist."

Gage gave me a wary smile. "Me too. Especially if that amulet is cursed. There's no telling if anyone else had it in their possession besides Petra."

"Do you think she died from the curse?" I was surprised he would have gone with that theory.

"I'm withholding judgment until we hear from EL. His report will be detailed, and with some good detective work, we'll discover she died from another reason that we can actually charge someone with."

Milo said, "I don't look good in stripes."

Thankfully, this time, only I heard his comment.

I picked him up and whispered in his ear, "Would you please watch what you're saying? You swore me to secrecy, not even to tell Gage. Here you are dropping hints, which Dax can overhear, that you're responsible for Petra's death."

He turned his head so he looked me in the eye. "Aren't I?"

"We don't know that yet. Stop jumping to conclusions." I placed him on the floor, carefully avoiding the shards of plastic. Even if it wouldn't cut his paws I wasn't about to test it.

Dax said, "I'm going to take one final look around just in case something was overlooked."

Milo trailed after him. His tail stuck straight up like an antenna.

Gage slipped his arm around my waist. "So, what are you holding back from me that Milo said before?"

"Nothing important. If you will give me a couple of minutes, I want to call Aunt Mimi and ask her about the poison, Devil's Hemlock."

He gave me a blank look. "Oh, you're talking about the poison book you were reading when I got to the shop?"

"Yes, based on Milo's symptoms, I think that could have been the culprit. But how it got on his fur is another question."

There were so many ideas floating around in my brain. I couldn't nail anything down to a specific cause of how Milo would have gotten a dangerous poison on his fur. Devil's Hemlock was hard to find. It was even harder to produce in some form that Milo wouldn't have recognized immediately.

"Go call your aunt. I can see this is important."

"How?"

He touched the spot between my eyes. "You get squiggle lines right here." He brushed his lips over mine. "It's always an indication that your brain is in overdrive. I'll be here when you're done."

I left the room and went into the main part of the library. It was filled with shadows compared to the annex, and I wondered if I should turn on the lights, but that might signal to people that it was actually open. We didn't need anyone coming in off the street and potentially contaminating the crime scene.

I pulled out a chair from the long oak table, sat down and dialed the phone. Aunt Mimi answered on the second ring.

"Lily, I was hoping you'd call."

"Hi, Aunt Mimi. I'm at the library with Gage, Dax, and Milo. We're looking for any clues to the break-in last night, and the removal of the Heart and Soul amulet." I heard her take in a deep breath and I knew exactly how she felt.

"Have you found anything useful yet?"

"Not really. Obviously we already knew that Petra had the amulet when she died. Dax cast a protection spell around it. For now, everyone is safe, but we need to find a permanent solution." I wished I could tell her that Milo might be the only one who could help us, but I held back.

"Well, that gives me some hope that we're not on the cusp of a tragedy."

A shudder raced over me as I agreed with her. When I got back to the bookstore, I would see what my book of magic could tell me about undoing a very bad curse cast by a former witch. "In other news, this morning, I was researching different poisons, and I came across Devil's Hemlock. It's deadly, and even in small amounts, if left untreated, the victim will die. It can be absorbed through skin contact or by inhaling it." I recalled the text exactly and continued, "The poison is a rare hybrid from Devil's Snare and Water Hemlock." I heard her take a sharp inhale.

"Lily, I know exactly what it does, and you might be right. Using that particular cleansing method you did last night, Milo reacted exactly the way he would if Devil's Hemlock was the poison. How is he today?"

"Drowsy, but his commentary is as sharp as ever."

"Bring him by, or better yet I'll come down to the bookstore. I'm sure you'd be calling me at some point today so that you can follow a clue or two. I'll check on him while I'm there."

I couldn't help but grin. My aunt knew me better than I knew myself. "Are you sure it won't be too much trouble?"

Her soft laughter soothed me. "I offered; you didn't ask. I'll be there in just over an hour."

"Thanks. That will be enough time to get back to the store and make notes on my clue board."

"See you shortly." She hung up. I knew she would give Milo a good check when she got to the Cozy Nook. I took a few minutes listening to the silence of the space. Peace wrapped around me. The sound of padding paws drew my attention.

"My dear witch, is everything okay?" Milo jumped into my lap, and I ran my hand the length of his body.

"I'm fine. I was taking a moment to appreciate all the wonderful things that have happened in my life. I realize last night it could have changed in a blink of an eye. Losing you would have devastated me."

He tapped my cheek with his paw, a gesture I had come to treasure. "But you didn't. You knew in your heart something was wrong, and you found me in time. I want to reassure you something like this has never happened to me before nor will it again. I have to believe I was in the wrong place at the wrong time."

"True. But it was good you were here to tell us who broke in last night and stole the amulet. We know Petra wanted it. Do you think she was able to leave the library with it and found her way to the beach where the curse overcame her?"

I didn't hear Gage come up behind us, and I jumped

when he said, "Petra Addington was poisoned, and get this, EL was doing some research, and at first he thought it was Water Hemlock, but then he thought it was Devil's Snare."

I knew exactly where he was headed. "It's Devil's Hemlock."

He placed his hand on my shoulder. "Sorry, I didn't mean to startle you. As soon as I heard the lab results I wanted you to know too."

"Did he say how it got into her system?"

EL's educated guess, it was sprayed on her face so she inhaled it into her lungs and absorbed it through her skin. With the double dose she would have died in an hour, give or take."

"I need to create a time line for the events last night but," I looked at Milo, "how did it get on you?"

Gage said, "If the poison was an aerosol and the murderer sprayed it in her face, and if Milo was close by, the overspray might have drifted in his direction."

"And without it being a larger dose, it took longer for him to be affected, which is why it didn't kill him too." I pulled Milo to my chest and squeezed him. "No more lurking. From now on you can prowl about, but don't stay in any one place too long. Got it?"

With a screech and a yowl, he pushed away from me. "I can't breathe, you're smothering me."

"Better smothered with love than something deadlier, my little man." I kissed the top of his soft, gray head and set him on the floor. "We need to get back to the store."

"I'm hoping there is some kind of treat when we do." He trotted in the direction of the exit door.

I stood and pushed the chair in. "Are you and Dax coming?"

Gage bobbed his head in the direction of the annex. "We'll be over in a couple of minutes. I want to make sure everything is locked up."

I made it as far as the door when I turned. He was too quick to stay behind. "Did you find something?"

"No. Why?"

With a shrug of my shoulders, I said, "No reason." I blew him a kiss and hurried out the door. I paused when I heard it click after me. I withdrew my phone and called the Coastal Motel. My first unknown was where the other four people involved in the break-in were staying. With some luck, they were still in town and willing to have a little chat with me.

I snapped my fingers. "Dang it. He's already had them brought down to the station for questioning. Since I'm here, I can't be lurking around the station trying to find out what was going on." I had to admire Gage. He was upping this investigation while keeping me safe. But two could play this game of chess. Then I had a sobering thought. I already was keeping a secret from him regarding this investigation. I needed to talk to Milo in private. There had to be some way to tell Gage the truth and protect my familiar from being implicated in a crime.

Chapter 8
Lily

I had called Nikki, who had been my best friend forever. She would be waiting for me at the bookstore when I got back. I jogged across the town square and was happy to see she was there and chatting with my mom. I rushed across the street.

"Hey, Mom. I wasn't expecting to see you today." I wrapped my arms around her and gave her a quick squeeze.

She patted the tote bag she had slung over her shoulder. "I had to deliver some tea to the restaurants in town and Bee Bee's Boutique, and while I was here, I thought I'd swing by to see if you and Gage would like to come for dinner this weekend." Her eyes held a glint of mischief. "Maybe we could talk about wedding plans?"

I waved my hand, and the door unlocked. Pushing it open I waited for Mom and Nikki to come inside. "I hope you brought tea to resupply me, too. It's always a great seller."

Nikki grinned. "She has a knack for the best blends in all the northeast."

My mom's cheeks flushed a deep shade of pink. "Stop. You girls should write advertising copy." She handed me her bag and dropped into a wingback chair with a sigh. "This chair is so comfy I could stay here all day."

I unpacked small white boxes of tea that bore the logo MRM Teas. I smiled. Mindy and Reed Michaels. An unlikely couple like me and Gage, but in this instance, my mom was non-magical, and Dad had put aside his magic to raise me to be like Mom. My magic had been suppressed until a year ago when my family's book of magic, *Practical Beginnings*, fell off a shelf and knocked me out. That's when I discovered Milo could talk. I sighed. So many wonderful things happened all because of that accident.

Nikki caught my eye. "Everything okay over there. That was a pretty heavy sigh coming from such a petite witch."

"Sorry. I took a quick stroll down memory lane, thinking about how much has changed in a short period of time." I crossed the room and set the tote bag next to Mom. "Coffee anyone?"

My mom got up. "I'll make it. Your phone is about to ring."

"How did you..." my words were interrupted by my phone.

"I might not be a witch but there are a few things I can do." She pointed to my cell phone. "Take your call. I'll be back shortly with three mugs of freshly brewed coffee."

I held out my hand, and the cell phone appeared in it. I didn't want the call to go to voice mail "Hello." I said breathless.

"Lily. It's Monica from the motel."

With a smile, I said, "Hi, Monica." I didn't bother to say I knew where she worked since she was the owner of the Coastal Motel and the name had come up on caller ID.

"Torrie asked me to give you a call. She is helping out the housekeeper today. We've been full all week, and you know the season hasn't even started yet. The college kids haven't come home, and I'm shorthanded."

"I appreciate the phone call, and please tell Torrie it's fine." I walked closer to where Milo had settled on the window seat. "I was hoping you could tell me if you have five people staying at the motel. They might be archeologists or maybe they'd be best described as the scholarly type."

"I only have three people who fit that generic description: two women and one man. They are in their late thirties. They were talking about that new exhibit at the Olde Town Library; at least, that's all I overheard when they were getting coffee this morning. I was expecting two more guests but they never showed."

That piqued my interest. "Did the three say they were going to the library this morning?"

"I think so. They were talking about a necklace or maybe they called it an amulet. I'm not sure. The phone rang, and I got busy. They hung around for a bit, and finally, they left. One of the women seemed annoyed as if they had been waiting for someone, but they hadn't shown up or called."

That sounded odd but promising. I kept my cool when I said, "Were they waiting for Petra?"

"No, they were waiting for a man. I'm not sure they

said the name. They just referred to a him, like he was late. That kind of comment."

That had to be Simon, which meant they knew Petra wouldn't be joining them. So, one of them; Donella, Roni, or Chaz had to be the killer. Or could it be Simon and he's in cahoots with the trio? I needed to come up with a better way to describe them even if it was just in my head.

"I'm sorry I couldn't be of more help Lily. I need to run, but if you think of anything else I can help with, you know where to find me."

After thanking her for the information, I disconnected and sat down next to Milo. Rubbing his soft gray fur always cleared my mind.

"My dear witch. What are you thinking?"

"I'm not sure what to do next. We really need to know how Petra Addington died."

"It was the amulet."

"Milo, I know you believe that to be true, but she wasn't wearing it. You've been emphatic on a couple of occasions that the person wearing it would succumb to death from the curse. Holding it is not the same thing."

He glared at me through narrowed eyes. "Whose amulet and curse is it?"

I scooped him up and kissed the top of his head. "I didn't mean to offend you. I'm sure you cast an amazingly powerful curse. I distinctly remember you saying when the person put it on, they would be doomed." Who knew a familiar could be so touchy about something he did a couple of hundred years ago? For that matter, I didn't even know how long a familiar would live.

"How did you become mine?" I could feel his body relax in my arms.

"That's easy. You needed the best familiar that walked on four paws, and it just so happened I had been waiting for you." He wriggled from me and stretched out on the window seat again.

"Like you had a feeling I was coming or you could see into the future?"

He rolled over on his back. "Why the sudden interest in how I came to be in Pembroke Cove when you were getting ready to find your furever best friend."

"I can ask Aunt Mimi." Would I be able to bluff him into revealing something about his past?

"You could." He did a deep kitty grumble, which meant he wasn't thrilled with me at this second. "Fine. But we're not about to get all sentimental. Understood?"

He had my full attention the moment he said "fine."

"My full name is Gabriel Milo," he cleared his throat, "Gabriel Michaels. I am your ancestor, who knew that one day there would be a Michaels witch destined to become as wise and powerful as me."

"And that's me?" My voice squeaked like a mouse.

He tipped his head as if assessing me. "Yes. After my unfortunate incident," he rubbed his paw over his face, "the witch who cursed me made me immortal not just a familiar. All I had to do was wait until the generations passed, and I found you. A witch I can teach all that I know."

My shoulders slumped. "We're related? For real? Who else knows about you?"

"Only you. I'm sure Phoenix suspects something since

we've spent a great deal of time together, and our family of witches are extraordinary."

I placed my hand over my heart. "I'm not. I can't even ride a broom yet."

"In due time, my dear witch. You've had a few murders to solve for Detective Cutie, and now another unfortunate incident has occurred, which you need to solve. I want to get my amulet back where it belongs."

"That's not going to be possible. Right now, it's evidence in a crime, and once it can be released by the police I'm sure whatever museum has acquired it will want it back."

"Stolen property doesn't belong in a museum." He swished his tail like it was a sword in battle.

Which was the perfect opening to discuss Gage. "Milo, I need to talk to you about something very important. Can you promise to keep an open mind?"

He gave me a side eye and finally said, "I don't know of any conversation in history that started that way which ended well."

With that point hitting the crux of this issue, I nodded. "It's about the amulet and you."

Now, with his full attention on me, I took a deep, calming breath. "I made a promise to you that I wouldn't share your connection to the amulet with anyone. Before there was a murder I fully intended to keep it."

"And now." The growl in his voice didn't mask his rising temper, and the slow movement of his tail confirmed it.

"I can't keep everything from Gage. At the scene of the crime last night, he almost touched the amulet. Even though you said a person had to wear it I hadn't wanted to take any chances with Gage's safety. I was able to prevent that until Dax arrived. He cast a protection spell that basically would make it harmless."

The silence hung between us. I had hoped Milo would understand and release me from my promise. If for no other reason than to keep Gage and the other people we care about safe from the curse.

"Lily, you do realize if you tell him anything about the curse, he'll have to know I'm a former witch who let another get the upper hand." He hung his head. "It's humiliating."

My heart ached for Milo. Being a Michaels witch was a big responsibility. I had only learned a fraction of what other members of my family knew, Milo included.

I ran my hand down the length of his body. "You're too hard on yourself, and Gage would never look at you differently."

Milo didn't lift his head. "Can I think about what we'll tell him? We'll do it tonight."

"You want to be there?" This was a new wrinkle. I thought he'd want to be anywhere but in the same room when I shared the information with Gage. "Does Aunt Mimi know who you are?"

"No. That can't change."

My brow furrowed. "I thought you said you felt that Phoenix guessed the truth."

His claws dug into the window seat. "Absolutely not. End of discussion." He vaulted from the cushion and disappeared around the side of a bookcase.

The breath escaped me, and my shoulders sagged. My mom crossed the room and rubbed my shoulder.

"Is Milo going to be okay? Your conversation seemed quite intense."

I nodded. "Yeah. He just needs some time to sort a few things out." I gave her a forced smile. "How about that coffee."

Nikki was sitting across from my usual wingback chair and my mom sat down. She pointed to the chair. "Stop chewing your bottom lip, and take a seat. Nothing will get resolved if you start pacing the store."

My clue board was blank, so I waved my hand, and the clues came into view.

Mom grinned. "You're very good."

I smiled at her compliment. "I'm better. I haven't plunged the town into darkness for a couple of months. Most of what I can do well is basic: unlock doors, light candles, you know, easy."

Nikki snorted. "Stop being modest. You found Milo last night when he was sick, and if you hadn't gotten there when you did, he would have died."

I let those words sink in. Milo would have died, but he said he was immortal. Now, those two statements don't jibe. I didn't want to add that to my clue board but why would Milo lie?

"What do we know at this point?" It was a rhetorical question, but I needed to stop dwelling on the Milo connection.

Mom rubbed her hands together. "This is the first time I've been involved with one of your cases."

Laughter bubbled up. "Don't let Gage hear you call it my case. He'd blow a gasket and would remind us all that I'm not a police officer and need to leave this investigation to the professionals."

"Well, I can see his point of view. The other cases you've worked on have brought you close to danger." She shuddered. I understood how much this would distress her.

"Mom, that's why Milo hounds me to read the book, *Practical Beginnings*. So far, it hasn't failed me. Besides, I have Nikki, who willingly comes along for the ride." I gave her a wink. "Most of the time."

"Mindy, if it wasn't for Lily, my wedding wouldn't have been nearly as memorable."

Thinking about her wedding on St. Patrick's Day had been the highlight of our year so far. Even if poor John Bailey had been discovered dead at the B & B. "Enough talking about the past." I tapped my chin, and the chalk hovered over the blackboard. I rattled off the names of my four suspects, "Add arrows to the word, motel. Add Milo at the bottom, 10:30 PM, and a question mark with poison next to it." Now the board was starting to come together. But we needed the information from the coroner to confirm how Petra died. Did she drown or from some other unknown cause? Her clothes were wet, but that had to have been from the tide.

9:00 PM - Petra Addington – Amulet
High heels, cursed amulet, right hand
Simon Beale
Roni Blake

Donella Hoffman
Chaz Tate
Paige Reed
Milo 10:30 PM – poison?

The door to the shop opened and Gage strode in with Dax beside him. For a split second, a pang pierced my heart. In a few short months, they had become more like brothers than coworkers. Gage would feel the loss when he worked cases after Dax began running the police department in Robins Pointe. It wasn't a matter of if he was going to take the job but when he would be moving.

Gage nodded to my clue board. "I have a tidbit for you. EL texted and made it official, Petra Addington died from a dose of Devil's Hemlock administered directly into her face. Based on the amount of poison in her system, it would have taken about an hour for her to succumb. EL's best educated guess, she had no idea what she had come in contact with was deadly and went to the beach. Maybe to savor having the Heart of the Soul amulet in her possession. It's possible she tried to wash her face in the salt water, and it was too late. Her face and hair were wet with salt water residue."

"Wouldn't that have been from the tide?"

"No. EL checked the tide charts. It would have reached the lower portion of her body but not her face. She was lucky high tide missed her." He frowned. "No, she wasn't lucky. Poor choice of words on my part."

Relief came in waves. "Wait until Milo learns the news. The curse didn't kill her." And that's when it dawned on me since Milo had gotten the overspray did his immortality give him an advantage and just get deathly ill? It didn't matter; all of these were important clues.

Milo slunk around the side of my chair. "Did someone say the curse didn't kill that awful woman?" I picked him up, grateful he was alive. He said, "I wonder why not?"

Chapter 9
Gage

From the moment I walked in the door, I scanned Lily's clue board. The details of Petra's death were neatly laid out in chronological order as we knew it at this point. Dax gave Milo a sharp look. It caused me to wonder what Milo had said. It really was annoying that I couldn't understand her familiar but there was nothing I could do. Despite our lack of communication, Milo had been instrumental in alerting me to the danger she was in after Archie Dane had been killed. I needed to believe if there was another time in the future he'd find a way to help.

"Mindy, it's nice to see you." I gave my future mother-in-law a warm smile. Her eyes held the same warmth as Lily's, and they had sable brown eyes, but that's where the similarity ended. Mindy was tall and willowy, whereas Lily was petite like her Aunt Mimi.

"Hello." Her smile included Dax, too. "I was delivering tea to a few stores and thought I'd pop in to see my beautiful daughter. I had no idea she was once again focused on a new murder case with you."

It wouldn't do any good to protest that she wasn't specifically working on a case with me. "Yes, unfortunately, we found the woman on the beach near the Clam Bake."

Mindy rose from the chair. "I'm going to leave you to the case and finish my deliveries." She crossed the room and kissed Lily's cheek. "Call me later."

Nikki said, "I'll walk you out. This looks serious, and if Lily needs me, she knows how to get in touch."

Lily held her mom tight, and when she released her, said, "Better still, meet me for lunch tomorrow. We can sit outside the bookstore and watch the world go by."

"That sounds nice. I'll bring a picnic if you provide the sunshine." She bent down and scooped Milo up. "And I'll have a special treat for you as well."

He purred loudly, and Lily grinned. "I can't control the weather, but Milo says he's already looking forward to it."

Nikki held the door as Mindy picked up her purse. "Everyone, stay safe, please." She pointed a finger at Lily. "And that means you too."

"Yes, Mom." She waited until the door was closed before spinning on her heel. "What else did you find out?"

I couldn't help but chuckle. "About the case?"

She tossed a paperback book at me, and I caught it midair. "Of course, the case."

I looked at the title of the book and said, "Poisons and Potions, A Beginners Guide." I quirked a brow in her direction. "Research?"

Her brows furrowed, and the line between them deepened. "What is this for?" She held out her hand, and I passed it back to her.

"Petra had a stack of books when she came to the

register and then put one aside before I could ring it up. This was it." She tapped her index finger to her chin. "I wonder why she changed her mind?"

"Why would an archeologist want a book on poisons?" Dax asked.

Milo snaked around her legs meowing loudly. Dax leaned forward, and he glanced at Lily. "This could be very serious."

I looked between Dax and Lily. "Can you share what Milo said?"

She said, "Remember how either Roni or Donella said they should leave the amulet alone? Based on the legend, it had been cursed and might not be safe. But Petra was determined to discover its secrets. Maybe she thought there was some residual poison on the gold and it would cause a reaction when touched."

"Or that she could extract some kind of power from it." I wasn't convinced the amulet was actually cursed. "Let's get back to the poison."

Lily had already listed it on the board. "What was Paige's role in this? Could she have left the side door unlocked so they could enter the library without actually breaking in?"

"I don't think we could have two disreputable librarians in Pembroke Cove. What would the odds be?"

Dax gave a snort. "Yeah, that would be pretty unlucky. I don't think we can take her off the suspect list just yet based on playing the odds."

Lily jabbed the chalk in his direction. "See, Dax understands where I'm coming from."

"You're right. She stays on the suspect list for now." I

paced in front of the clue board. "Let's review what we know so far about everyone involved."

Dax pulled out his phone. "I've been digging around. Petra Addington was a respected archeologist. However, her reputation for human interaction is the opposite. It seems she didn't care who she trampled over in her quest to be the very best in her field."

"Did she have a scope of interest?" Lily asked.

"She specialized in jewelry and has published several papers on the importance of gems over the centuries. It's not surprising that she would be fascinated with the lore of the Heart of the Soul amulet. When it was first discovered approximately one hundred and fifty years ago, the legend had been handed down. That it was cursed by the original wizard that owned it many years before that."

I watched Lily's brow arch, but the rest of her face was a mask. "How so?"

"According to my research, the necklace was crafted by a wizard to protect the people who came to him for guidance and help. Until the wizard's rival lay claim to it, killing the wizard in the process. It said that before the wizard perished, he cursed the opal so that anyone who wore it would die."

"Where did you come across these details? When I did a cursory search, nothing like that came up."

Dax gave Lily a quick look, but she remained silent. What was going on between these two?

"After Lily asked me to put a protection spell around the amulet, I called my mother and had her look into the coven archives."

"Lily, is there something you want to tell me?"

Milo leaped from the floor into her arms and began to meow. Lily was nodding and she avoided Dax's stare.

I couldn't question Milo but Lily was a different story. She was hiding something, and it was relevant to the murder. I didn't need to speak familiar to know that.

"Okay, here it is but I don't want you to get mad." Milo reached up and patted her cheek as if he was giving her comfort. "But you have to promise that you won't look at Milo any differently?"

"I get that you two are bonded, but if you or Milo knows something about Petra's murder, you have to tell me." I took a step toward them, and Milo hissed at me. I held up my hand. "Milo, I promise nothing will change." Slowly, his body returned to a relaxed position in Lily's arms. I was no longer in danger of being scratched.

Lily focused her attention on Dax. "Can you wait outside?"

His mouth gaped open, and he took a step to the door until Milo's growl stopped him. "Are you sure, Milo? I can wait outside?"

Another few meows from Milo, and Dax returned to where we stood.

"What I'm about to say can't leave this shop." Lily exhaled a deep breath and said, "At one time Milo was a powerful witch. The Heart of the Soul amulet was his. Some of the stories are correct, but he wasn't a wizard, and before he was turned into a familiar, he cursed it. Which is why he was sitting outside the library when Petra and her associates went inside. He was doing all he could to protect it so it wouldn't cause harm."

I sank into a chair. This would take some processing.

Silence threatened to overwhelm me. Questions sprang to mind that didn't make sense.

"How long have you known about Milo?" That seemed as good a place as any to start.

"He told me after Petra left the store. It was only when he saw the books they had and overheard Simon talking with her that he knew the potential for trouble."

Hurt and annoyance were warring inside of me. Why had it taken her so long to tell me? If she had been up front, some of the investigations would have gone more quickly. "Why didn't you tell me when we found her on the beach? Instead, you used Dax's magic to protect me and everyone else." I whirled in the chair and faced him. "Did you know?" I shook my head. "Of course you didn't, or Lily wouldn't have asked you to leave the store."

She said, "Milo swore me to silence. He was embarrassed, and in his defense, he never thought the amulet posed any real danger, as long as she didn't put it on."

"That didn't work out very well for Petra. She died." I tried hard to keep my tone even, but it was a struggle.

Lily sat next to me and placed Milo on the floor. "Look. I wanted to tell you, but Milo asked me to keep his confidence. It was only before you arrived today that he agreed I could share this with you."

I couldn't fault her loyalty to Milo. It was one of her best qualities that I admired. It hadn't been that long since we discovered the murder. I had to ask, "Is there anything I should be made aware of before I continue my investigation?"

"No, other than what you know. He came in contact with the poison while standing guard at the library."

"Did he tell you that was his plan?" I ran my hand down Milo's back hoping to reassure him that on some level I understood why he did what he had.

"About his stake out, no. Remember when we got back to my place he wasn't there. It was only after you left that I tried to do the location spell without success then I used the connection spell that works between witch and familiar and went looking for him."

She shuddered, and I wrapped my arm around her, kissing her temple. I said, "I'm sorry he got caught up in all of this, but if you had given me a heads-up, I could have put security on the library, and maybe it wouldn't have happened."

Lily pulled away and stared at me, open-mouthed. Standing up she said, "You're going to blame me for a criminal act. The exhibit was protected by library security and locked cases. Just because Petra was overzealous with her desire to get her hands on it is not my fault. Furthermore, she could have pitched her case to her superiors, whoever they might be, and push to be the person who examined it before anyone else. I don't know how this process works with museums."

Dax looked between the two of us. "Gage. You're being a little harsh on Lily. There is one sacred bond in our covens, which is the bond between Lily and Milo. I'm sure she knew Milo would come around, but he needed some time to come to terms with what had happened. Milo has been carrying this burden with him for a long time."

"In more ways than one." Milo gave me a head butt, and he hissed at me. "What did I say that was out of line?"

Lily had her arms folded over her chest, and she tapped

the toe of her shoe on the floor. The tapping against the wood floor grew in volume with each tap. "You were rude. With the way you said it, not what you said. Are you trying to insinuate he's old?"

My favorite witch was definitely touchy about this entire topic. "What I meant was Milo has been carrying the burden of what happened to him and what he did for a long time. That is a heavy weight to have borne alone."

Her face softened. "Now you understand. Not that any of this really helps the case since Devil's Hemlock is what killed her, not the curse."

Milo meowed.

Dax said, "Good point. The curse couldn't be responsible since she was holding the necklace and not wearing it. But who administered the poison and what was the delivery method?"

"If Milo also received a dose we have to assume it was in aerosol." I picked up the chalk. "Do we know if any of the remaining four have a chemistry background, like a secondary degree that would point us in a new direction?"

"I have called each of their employers except for Simon Beale since he worked for Petra. I have contacted her employer, too. I don't expect to get much from that thread since she worked for a private organization that brokered acquisitions for private collectors. On the surface, it seems her focus and determination, we saw on full display at the library, would be an asset for the private sector, and there is certainly more money in that endeavor."

"Good work, Dax. When do you think we'll hear back?"

"With any luck, later today. Until then, we need to

bring everyone into the police station again and see if we can get anything out of them." He looked at Lily. "So far, they're being pretty tight-lipped."

"Maybe it's time that I bump into them. It's possible I might have more luck since my approach will be from the angle, I found her. Express my sympathy. You know all the important stuff from one human to another."

As much as I hated to admit to Lily that she was right, this was a good way to try and obtain information. It would put her squarely in the killer's line of sight. That is one thought that sent chills down my spine. "Before I agree..." her face lit up like sunshine in July. "There has to be conditions you must follow."

She beamed and nodded so hard I thought her head might pop off. "You have to see if Nikki will go with you."

Chapter 10
Lily

The next morning, I sat on the bench at the edge of the town square, close to the police station. I needed time for my brain to clear, and from this vantage point, I could see most of the entrances to the shops and restaurants. I kept watch for Nikki and my four suspects. With any luck, they'd come into town and would either go to Robin's Café or the Copper Kettle for breakfast. I had called in a favor of Monica, who was the owner of the Coastal Motel. After explaining the situation, I asked if she could conveniently say the coffee pot wasn't working and the pastries hadn't been delivered this morning for the continental breakfast. In return, she could offer them fifteen percent off coupons to one of the cafes in town. That had been an hour ago. I had my fingers and toes crossed that they'd come into town and not head up Route One to Robins Pointe for breakfast.

My gaze drifted to the library and the general location where I had discovered Milo. Today, I was going back over there to find some evidence of how he had become the victim of the poison, and we also needed to have a chat about his life expectancy. He had said when the witch cursed him, it had been for eternity, so why did he almost die? I snapped my finger and sat up straight on the bench. A thought had been churning in my brain, and finally, I knew what it was. In the coven we belong to, our motto is to do no harm. Why on earth would Milo have cursed the amulet with revenge for whoever wore it? That was directly against our guiding principles.

From the corner of my eye, I noticed Nikki coming out of The Sweet Spot. Bless the stars, she was carrying a small white bag and a cardboard tray with two to-go mugs resting in it.

Nikki grinned. "Hey, I thought since we're on a stakeout we should have something to keep us fueled."

I snorted. "I don't know if this qualifies as a stakeout." I gestured for her to take a seat and smiled as I took the coffee. "This does add to our cover story that we're simply two friends enjoying a cup of coffee on a beautiful morning."

She set the white bakery bag between us. "I grabbed a couple of blueberry muffins, easier to eat than cinnamon buns."

Just the mention of my favorite treat from William's bakery made my stomach grumble, but the muffins were excellent too. "As Milo would say, you're my favorite witch."

She laughed softly as she scanned the grassy area. "Nothing yet?"

"No, but I had Monica tell them her delivery didn't

arrive, and the coffee pot was on the fritz, so they'll have to eat somewhere, and I'm hoping they don't head north."

Sipping our coffee, we watched and made small talk about the upcoming sandcastle competition in June, which brought in the early tourist crowd. The minutes dragged by, and with a quick glance at my watch, I realized it was almost time to open the store. "I'm only going to give our semi-stakeout ten more minutes."

Nikki smiled behind her coffee cup. "You won't need ten, look at the group of three people coming out of the B & B."

Sure enough, headed in our direction were Donella, Roni, and Chaz. I grabbed the white bag and stood. "I'm going to bump into them. Are you coming?"

"Heck yes." Matching my stride, Nikki and I hurried across the grass and down the brick sidewalk.

"Good morning," Nikki said.

The women slowed their steps, and Chaz did the same.

"Hello." Chaz paused and acknowledged me. "You're the woman who owns the bookstore."

"Yes, Lily Michaels and this is Nikki Twing-Jones."

Roni's eyes widened. "Is it true that you found Petra with the police officer?"

I could hear the curiosity in her tone and didn't get the vibe she was saddened to have learned the news. "Yes, Detective Erikson and I were having dinner and went for a walk along the beach. That's where we found her."

"Was it shocking? You know, to find a real dead body?"

The gleam in her eye was definitely morbid curiosity. I wasn't going to fuel her ideas by telling her this wasn't my first. "Finding her was not what I had been expecting, but I was surprised to see she had the Heart of the Soul amulet with her. Do you have any idea how she got it from the library?"

Donella licked her lips, and her eyes darted to Chaz and then to Roni. For a moment, I thought no one was going to answer my question.

Chaz said, "Paige Reed and I were friends in college. When she learned the exhibit was passing through Pembroke Cove, she got in touch with me. There would be fewer crowds here where my colleagues and I could get an up-close look at it."

I cocked my head to the side. "Like she was going to give you access to it?"

He shook his head. "Nothing like that. Paige is by the book, no pun intended."

Roni chimed in, "But she wouldn't hurry us out at the end of the day so we could take pictures, measurements, through the glass, of course. You know, really look at it. When Petra discovered us here, she was furious. Accused us of using Paige to gain an unfair advantage. You see, we needed to submit a proposal to even be considered a part of the team that was going to do a deep dive into the origins of the amulet and its supposed power." She leaned forward. "It's rumored to bring death to whoever wore it. But that was years ago. Once it became part of the museum in Salem it's been secured in a vault where no one could see it, let alone touch it."

Donella said, "That all changed four days ago."

Nikki said, "What happened?"

Roni nodded to Donella who picked up the explanation. "We were in Salem examining other artifacts recently discovered on a dig in Wethersfield. They're believed to be that of a coven there. But upon close examination, they are from the Wongunk Tribe. A true find but not what we had been hoping to discover."

"We focus on jewelry such as amulets," Chaz said.

Their story was winding around a bend, and I needed to bring it back into the moment. "If you were in Connecticut, why come to Maine?"

"As you can imagine, the circle of people who are in our field is rather small, and we've known Simon for a very long time, even before he started to work for Petra. He called to let us know that they were coming to Pembroke Cove with the intent to take the lead on this once-in-a-lifetime project."

I chewed the corner of my bottom lip. They didn't know the case was constructed of plastic which was interesting. "Why would Simon call you? As we all know, he worked for Petra."

"True but she treated him like a servant, not as a knowledgeable person on the team. Everything was about Petra, and if she got the opportunity to write this paper, the name Simon Beale would never appear in conjunction with it."

"Why didn't he just quit working with her." I would never understand why anyone would want to work for someone they didn't like or respect.

Chaz gave a snort. "Are you kidding? Jobs like this don't come along every day. It's better to suffer with an egomaniac than to be working an information desk at the museum." Donella and Roni nodded as he spoke.

With this background information, I had to ask, "Do

you think Simon finally got tired of being her lackey and killed her?"

Roni didn't blink or hide the contempt in her voice as she said, "I wouldn't blame him if he did. She was a vile woman."

Chaz hissed, "Hush. Don't spread vicious gossip since he could do the same back at us. Besides, he will be coming out of the B & B any minute to join us for breakfast."

Roni looked over her shoulder in the direction of the front door as if waiting for Simon to come out on cue. "Look, I hope you don't have the wrong idea about us. It's not our fault she was found dead holding on to that necklace for dear life. But she wasn't wearing it; therefore, if it was cursed as the legend said, the curse didn't kill her. Probably a random act of violence."

I felt my brows skyrocket to my hairline. How did she know she wasn't wearing it since I had only said it was in her possession? "So how do you think she got the amulet out of the library?" I looked at Roni, Chaz, and Donella one at a time, giving a pointed look, hoping to see a flicker of something, maybe guilt, in their eyes.

Roni's face flushed with color. "We all met at the library to see if we could find a way to get a better look at it, but when we discovered the case was secured, the three of us left, leaving Simon and Petra to head back to the inn, and we went to the motel."

The first crack in their alibi. Milo had seen them together, and I would take his word over anyone's.

The sound of a door closing drew my attention to the inn. Simon came whistling down the porch steps. His pace slowed when he saw Nikki and I talking with the others.

"Hello." He looked at his friends. "What's going on here?"

Roni slipped her arm through his. "We were just talking to Lily about Petra; you remember, she runs the bookstore. She found her, and I'm sure it's been a help talking with us. Reassuring her that although we feel bad about what happened, we weren't involved."

I could feel Nikki looking at me as Roni was quick to deflect their real involvement.

"Simon, I'm sorry for your loss. It must be hard to lose someone you've worked closely with for..." I let that hang to see if he'd fill in the blank.

"It is. I've worked with Petra for over ten years. It's a shame that the one object she was obsessed with ultimately was her downfall."

Donella nodded. "A thought occurred to me. Do you know when the amulet will be released back to the display? There is still that proposal due at the end of the month. Now there is less competition to submit a paper. Who knows, if the four of us collaborate, we could actually be the big winners."

I took a step back. Wow, these people were cold-hearted. Petra's body hadn't even been released to the next of kin for burial, and they were already picking over her life's work if they were to be believed. "That's a question you'll need to ask Detective Erikson. It's evidence in the investigation."

Chaz said, "We should get going to breakfast. Do you ladies have a recommendation for the best place to eat?"

Nikki said, "You can't go wrong with Robin's Café or the Copper Kettle."

Simon shifted from one foot to the other and looked me in the eye. "There was one additional copy of the book Petra bought on the subject of amulets. Do you still have it? It's secured in her room, and that woman police officer said everything was evidence."

Understanding he needed reference material I said, "I'm sure I do. Would you like me to put it aside for you?"

He nodded. "Thanks. I'll stop by later if that's okay."

"Of course. I'm open until five."

"Good." He said, "If you are ready, let's go eat. We can talk about something other than the last few days."

I swear Roni batted her eyelashes as she tightened her arm around his. "I'm sure you must need a distraction."

As the group walked away, I heard Chaz say, "We need to get our hands on the amulet if we still plan to submit the proposal at the end of this week."

Simon glanced back at Nikki and me, and I swore he winked at me. What the heck was all that about?

Watching them, I returned to my earlier plan. "Are you in a hurry to get home and start baking?" I was sure Nikki had bakery orders to fulfill for the restaurants in the area.

"I have time. What do you want to do?"

"I need to take a look around the grounds of the library and look under the bushes where I found Milo. With any luck, we'll find a clue before we go inside and talk with Paige." I drank the last of my now-cool coffee. "I find it interesting that she never mentioned she knew anyone in this little band of archeologists."

Nikki tossed her cup in a nearby garbage can and did the same with mine. "Paige seems so nice. You don't think she's caught up in this mess, do you?"

"It's not the first time a librarian hasn't been what they appeared to be." For a moment, my thoughts drifted to Flora Gray and how she had been extorting money from people in town. I sure hoped we didn't have another rotten apple in our midst. "However, there's only one way to find out, and that is to spend a bit of time chatting her up."

Nikki rubbed her hands together and grinned. "At least this time it's a public place so we shouldn't need to worry about confronting a suspected killer."

I gave her a side glance. "Are you forgetting the first time I cast a protection spell was in that very building?"

She shrugged her shoulders. "I forgot. But look on the bright side. Your witchy skills have gotten so much better since then, and we'll be together."

I laughed. "Are you asking me what could go wrong?"

She grinned. "Yeah, well what could go right? You can find a clue that breaks this case wide open, and Gage will be thrilled to arrest the guilty party and close the book on it."

"Nik, if only it were that easy. I'm afraid right now, we have four, maybe five, strong suspects, and my intuition isn't guiding me in any direction. Let alone ready to solve the case."

"Then we'd better get busy looking for clues." She glanced around the empty street, withdrew her wand, and with a flick, she was holding an oversized magnifying glass. With a gleam of laughter in her eye, she said, "Maybe this will come in handy."

I slipped my arm around her waist and laughed even louder. "Thanks, but I don't think that will be necessary."

"No problem." With a tap of her wand on the metal, it disappeared.

With a pep in our step, we crossed the grassy patch as we walked to the library. I was surprised to see Paige hurrying up the front steps as the clock in the town hall chimed ten. More to myself than to Nikki I said, "I wonder why she's running late?"

Chapter 11
Lily

"Paige!" In the short time she had been head librarian, I noticed the world clock could be set to her arrival and departure from the library. She pushed open the door and looked over her shoulder as she disappeared inside.

I ran up the steps and strode into the lobby. Her desk was on a four-inch raised platform in the middle of the room, but she wasn't behind it. "Nikki, you take the exhibit space, and I'll go into the back. I can't imagine why she ignored us."

We split off, and I hurried around tables in the general direction of the back office while looking down the rows of bookshelves. I even ducked into the community room, but she was nowhere to be found. Hopefully, Nikki had bumped into her.

I moved in the direction of the exhibit space when I heard a sniffle. It was muffled, followed by the sound of someone crying. I briefly thought of using a locator spell, but following the clues might be beneficial to the case.

Pausing to listen more closely, I moved down one row in the direction of the children's section.

There was a half wall with pint-sized bookshelves separating it from the larger library. The space was kid-friendly, with oversized floor pillows for lounging, small wooden tables and chairs, and even a few rocking chairs. There was Paige, curled into a fetal position on one of the floor pillows. Her face was buried in her hands as her shoulders racked with sobs.

I drew closer to her and dropped to the floor, placing a gentle hand on her shoulder. "Paige, what's wrong?"

A muffled "Nothing" was her response.

"Paige, nobody starts their day crying in the kids' section of the library if everything is rainbows and unicorns."

She looked at me through a V she made in her fingers. "How would you know? Your life is wonderful." The tears began again.

"How about a cup of tea and we can talk about whatever has you so upset."

"Why?"

"Tea helps everything."

Nikki came around the corner and her eyebrow quirked. "Lily?"

"We're going to have tea. Would you care to make us some and then come on back? Paige is having a rough start, and I think she could use some friends with her."

"I'm on it." She stepped back, giving me the space to get Paige in a chair while she conjured up a teapot and cups. I didn't think in Paige's state of mind she'd realized how it came to be.

I slipped my hand under her elbow. "Let's get comfortable in a chair." Although I was doubtful how comfy a kiddie chair would be. Paige was agreeable to getting off the floor. That was a step in the right direction. Once she was sitting in a chair, I magicked a packet of tissues from my pocket and handed them to her. She gave me a forced smile and said thank you.

As her breathing returned to a normal rate, Paige dabbed her red-rimmed eyes and blew her nose. "I must look awful."

"No, you don't. You look like a woman in need of friends."

She looked at the floor. "A friend is what got me into this mess."

Nikki came around the corner carrying a wooden tray with a floral china teapot and three dainty cups. "I found this in the community room. I hope it's okay that I used it."

Paige's eyes grew round. "I had no idea that was in there, but it's very pretty. It must have been a donation before I started."

I gave Nikki a wink. That was excellent thinking on her part. "It's been around for ages."

Nikki placed the tray on the small table and each of us fixed our cup and then sipped in silence. It was best to give Paige time to organize her thoughts. I really wanted to jump on that comment about friends. "This is nice."

She glanced at me over the rim of the cup. "What are you doing here so early? Don't you need to open the Cozy Nook?"

"It can wait. I think you're in need of us more than selling a book or two."

"Lily, why are you being so nice to me? We barely know each other."

"True. Are you saying I should have ignored the fact that you're upset? Sorry, no can do." I placed a hand on her arm and gave it a gentle squeeze. "I..." I glanced at Nikki. "We might have been remiss in reaching out and welcoming you into the community, but we're here now."

Paige's smile seemed to grow with each word I spoke. "Thank you." She turned her head to look out the window. "You might change your mind when you know what I've done."

My heart rate ticked up. Was she about to confess to helping Petra steal the amulet? Or worse. "We won't. We're here to help you in any way we can."

"About a week ago, an old friend called and said he was coming to town to see the exhibit."

She didn't need to elaborate on what exhibit. This was a rare occurrence to have something so cool come to Pembroke Cove. "How exciting." I didn't know what else to say. It sounded lame to my ears, but at least it broke the silence and might encourage her to keep talking.

She looked at me. "To be honest, I wasn't surprised; Charlie had always been fascinated by anything that reportedly had magic."

"Charlie?"

"Charles Tate. Oh wait, he goes by Chaz now." She shrugged her shoulders. "I guess it sounds more interesting than Charlie."

I needed to keep her on track. Nikki said, "Did he want to get together when he arrived?"

"Yes and no. He was bringing his co-workers with him

and asked if I would allow them to have a special viewing. I didn't think it would hurt anything, so I agreed. After the exhibit opened, I gave them access one evening. That was the night Petra was killed." She took a gulp of tea. "I left the side door open for them to come in, and it was agreed when they left, I could come back and secure the building. You have to believe me. I planned on coming back, taking a look around to make sure everything was in order, and then lock up."

"What happened?"

Tears hovered on her bottom lashes. "Charlie never called so I assumed they changed their minds. It wasn't until the next morning that I knew they had been here, and not only that but the Heart of the Soul was gone. By leaving the door open, I allowed someone to stroll in here and steal it."

I wanted to share all the details of that night, but she was still a suspect even if my gut was saying she hadn't been directly involved in the theft or Petra's death. "When did you learn about the theft?"

"Yesterday morning when I got to work. There were police officers everywhere. It's our late day since we stay open until eight. That's when I heard the amulet had been stolen and, of course, that Petra had it in her possession." She placed her hand over her lips and muffled the next words, "When she was found."

I leaned forward in my chair. "Did you know Petra Addington?"

She slowly shook her head. "Not until the day she and her assistant showed up."

"When they all met at the exhibit?"

Her eyes bulged. "No. She and Mr. Beale came to the library the day before the exhibit opened. She demanded to get early access, but the museum officials were adamant. No one, not even me, had early access."

"What happened with Petra when you refused?"

"She got huffy and left. I didn't see her again until the next day. That was when Chaz and his friends arrived. The five of them were in there together. Then you arrived, and I heard people arguing, and Chaz and the ladies stormed out. But before he left, he gave me a wink as if to remind me to leave the side door unlocked."

"And you didn't come back until the next morning?" Nikki asked.

"Nope. I mean, I should have, but what could happen in this quaint little town?" The teacup rattled against the saucer as she set her empty cup down.

I was not going down that rabbit hole and scaring this poor woman with everything that had happened before she arrived. "Bad things can happen anywhere, Paige, and don't beat yourself up that you didn't come back. You could have interrupted Petra when she was stealing the amulet, and things might have gone badly from there."

Her face paled. "I never thought of that. But do you think Detective Erikson will want to talk to me again? I may have left out a few details that I just shared with you."

I got up and stretched my arms overhead after sitting in the little wooden chair. "Paige, you need to call Gage and see if he can come by. You have to tell him everything."

"Will he arrest me for lying?" The quiver in her voice was getting more distinct.

I leaned down and hugged her. "He won't arrest you,

and you'll feel better once you talk to him. If you want, we can stay with you."

"No. I'll be fine. Just talking with you has been a huge help." She got up and pulled out her cell phone. "Do you have his number?"

I rattled off the digits and motioned for Nikki to follow me. We needed to do a quick search of the exhibit room and then head outdoors to look around. Then, I had to get back to the bookstore and add the new information to my clue board.

When Paige tucked her phone into her skirt pocket she gave me a wide, albeit forced, smile. "Thanks for everything, ladies. Detective Erikson said he'd be over in a few minutes."

Nikki said, "Lily has something she needs to do, but I'll stay here until he comes."

Seizing the opportunity, I slipped out of the room. Paige was in good hands, and I knew what I wanted to see. I eased open the annex door. The lights came on automatically, illuminating the silent, cavernous space. I walked around the perimeter of the room saving the actual display case of where the amulet should be for last. There wasn't so much as a dust mote on the floors, and everything seemed to be in order. I reached the display case where the amulet should be. There was a perfectly cut hole in the plastic, large enough for a hand to reach in. I closed my eyes and pictured someone using a scribe to score the glazing and then pop out a piece like they did in the movies. But was Petra skilled to do that, or was Simon? What about one of the others? Based on Milo's observation, they were together when they came out of the library. I looked around one more time. There wasn't anything more to see. Next, was to examine the outside of the library, especially where I discovered Milo. I was convinced I'd find something, even if it was small. There had to be a clue since I needed to discover who had hurt Milo as well as killed Petra.

Gage and Dax were inside talking with Paige, so Nikki and I left them to talk. I knew Gage wouldn't be thrilled that Paige hadn't been forthcoming the first time he questioned her, but at least now he'd have all her information.

I walked carefully down the stone steps, my eyes focused on each groove.

Nikki asked, "What do you think you're going to find?"

I shook my head. "I'm not sure. I have to try to find something." I pointed to the side door. "Let's head over there. I don't think they came down these steps but used that to enter and exit since it was partially hidden from the street." It was also where I found Milo.

I retraced the path that I thought Petra would have taken that night. "Nikki, stand over here." I steered her to where I found Milo. "You're going to be Milo so can you crouch down?"

She said, "Want me to turn myself into a cat so I can get the kitty view?"

My eyes widened. "You can do that?"

With a laugh, she said, "Let me guess you, haven't read that part of your book yet?"

"Nope and one feline in my family is enough. But don't turn yourself into a cat. Just kneeling down will be suffi-cient." She did as I asked.

"I'm going to pretend like I've come from the side door and down the path, turning in your direction. Keep your eyes on the ground as I'm moving and let me know if you see anything."

She tapped two fingers to her eyebrow. "Got it, Holmes."

"You know Dr. Watson would never have agreed to pretend, let alone offer, to be a cat. You're a much better partner than he ever was."

She meowed, and I laughed. It also took the edge off the seriousness of our task. I knew I was putting pressure on myself, but it was critical to find something. At this point, other than our suspects, I was no closer to figuring out who killed Petra. The why, the amulet. The how, poison, but who made it, when, and who was the intended victim?

I started at the door and very slowly made my way down the path, my eyes glued to the ground as I looked from right to left and back. Other than a stray gum wrapper, which, of course, I picked up and checked before tossing it into the garbage can, there was nothing until I walked around the back of Nikki. On the ground was a small green cylinder. I stooped to pick it up and paused to pull gloves from my pocket. Then, before I touched it, I used my phone to take a bunch of pictures like I had seen Sharon Peabody do countless times.

When I was satisfied I had taken enough photos, I snapped my gloves on. "Nikki, look at this."

I pointed to the container. It was about four inches long and half as wide. I wanted to pick it up. Instead, I stepped back and withdrew my book, Practical Beginnings, from my shoulder bag. I placed my hand on the well-worn black leather cover and closed my eyes.

"Show me a spell that will reveal if this container I found contains poison." I removed my hand and supported the underside as the pages fluttered in the late morning breeze. Finally, it stayed open on one page. I looked up. Nikki was standing in front of me with a grin.

"Nicely done."

"Thanks." I read the spell silently before asking her to hold it open to this page. I didn't have time to commit it to memory.

"If this cannister can harm thee, I call on the power of three. Flip it over thrice, for this, I wish so shall it be." No sooner had the words left my mouth than it rolled from me three times.

My mouth gaped open and I looked at Nikki. "So now what do I do?"

Chapter 12
Gage

After Lily left the library I thanked Paige for the information about my suspects. My cell buzzed with an incoming text. With a quick glance at Dax, I said, "We need to go. Now."

He never asked a question; he just fell into step beside me as our pace brought us to the front door in record time. Once we were outside I scanned the area until my eyes found Lily and Nikki. "There."

We jogged down the steps, and she held her hand up to stop us from getting too close. "Sorry to interrupt you with Paige, but this is important." She pointed to a small green canister on the ground, half covered in some grass clippings. "Don't touch it. But I believe that tiny canister is how the Devil's Hemlock was dispersed."

"You know this, how?" I was cautious and wished she had more space between her and the canister. I didn't know much about poisons that were a magical combination, but since Dax wasn't freaking out, I figured there was some measure of safety. The only reason I knew it was a non-magical combination was Dax mentioned it earlier today. How a non-magical got their hands on it was a huge question mark. But did Lily know what it really was?

Her eyes went wide as she crossed her arms over her midsection. "For the record, I didn't touch it. However, I cast a spell when I discovered it. Just to be safe."

Nikki nodded. "Neither of us did. But how are you going to take it into evidence and have it confirmed by a lab that this was the murder weapon? It's lethal."

Dax had pulled out an evidence bag, from where I didn't ask or really care. "I think we'll need that to be doubled. Just in case it gets punctured."

"Consider it done." He looked at Nikki and Lily. "If you can stand on either side, and we'll create a shield. I can get it into the bag without touching it."

"Magical camouflage?" Lily asked. "Good idea."

"Yes." He knelt on the ground close to the small canister. It reminded me of a perfume atomizer and said, "Go for it."

Lily and Nikki said some words very softly and nothing seemed to change until Dax stood and zipped the bag closed. It was a seamless transfer, and if anyone had happened to see us, they wouldn't have realized that Dax never touched it.

"We'll get this to EL, and he can arrange for it to be handled with the utmost care. I'm going to suggest a face mask and heavy-duty chemical gloves." Dax waved a hand over the bag and gave me a reassuring smile. "I've added an industrial strength protection spell as well. It won't interfere with the identification but it will protect all involved."

"Good." I didn't want anyone else to become collateral

damage with this recent discovery. "Thanks for convincing Paige to talk with me. She didn't give me much more than I already knew, but I think she's still hiding something."

Lily said, "She told you about her previous friendship with Chaz Tate?"

I didn't want to have this conversation in the middle of the town square. "Can we head over to the store?"

"Sure." Lily extended her hand to me and I took it.

We crossed the grassy area hand in hand and I tugged her close to my side. Dax and Nikki were with us.

"I'm glad you were extra careful when you found that atomizer. You've really grown into this amateur sleuth role that you insist on pursuing. Even if I wish you wouldn't, you're being careful, and that's all I've ever asked."

"I've never knowingly put myself in danger; just a couple of times it worked out that way."

I kissed her cheek as I absorbed her strength and calmness at the same time. "You're amazing."

With a movement of her hand from right to left, I knew she had unlocked the door to her bookstore, and we entered. Milo greeted us with several deep meows. She released my hand and knelt down to pick him up.

"Hi to you too."

He meowed again as she ran her hand over the length of his back a few times. "I'm fine, and so is Nikki. And yes, to your unasked question, we have some very good information, including finding the item used to dispense the poison." She shuddered, and I wrapped my arms around the two of them.

"Everyone is safe now, Milo." He turned his deep green eyes to me and grumbled.

Lily laughed and placed him on a wingback chair. "What did he say?"

Dax and Nikki just smiled. Lily cupped my cheek in the palm of her hand. "He pointed out I made, the big find, as he called it. In addition, he said you should be commended for having the good sense to fall in love with a Michaels witch."

With a snort, I said, "I had the good sense to fall in love with you long before I knew you were one. Heck, before you even knew you were a witch, either. I guess that makes us both brilliant."

With a peck on my lips, Lily said, "Coffee?"

I rubbed my hands together and said, "I'll get the clue board."

Dax turned the two extra chairs around so they'd be facing the wingback chairs and the board. I retrieved the board from the small closet near the coffee pot in the back room. My thoughts were whirling. When I set the board up, I said, "Dax, did you ever find out which of the four suspects had a degree in chemistry?"

He sat down and rested an ankle over the opposite knee. "Yes. But you're not going to like it."

My gut told me I already knew the answer, it was either none or all. "You might as well wait for Lily to come back."

Nikki had joined her and was carrying out slices of coffee cake while Lily brought in the coffee tray. We had spent many days sitting around talking about town happenings before Lily became a witch. There were days I missed that, but it was less isolating having her be a part of my everyday world too. Of course, when Dax left for Robins Pointe, we'd be a trio.

"What did I miss?" Lily placed the tray on the side table and glanced at the board. She seemed satisfied the clues were as she had left them.

"Dax discovered something about who might hold a degree in chemistry."

She handed out mugs of coffee as she gave him an expectant look.

He kept his voice monotone as he said, "Simon, Chaz, and Roni obtained minors in chemistry; Donella majored in it."

Lily dropped to the chair and propped her chin in her hand. "That doesn't narrow things down at all, and why would Donella have a degree in chemistry and work in archeology? Don't you find that a bit odd?"

I picked up the chalk and added a star for the minor degrees and two stars for the major next to each of their names. Then, next to Paige's name, I added Chaz Tate, friends.

"What about Paige?"

Dax nodded with a grin and said, "Excellent question. Since she and Chaz were friends, did they have that particular class together? The answer is no. She was an English major, and she got her master's in library science. She's a word nerd to the core."

Lily glanced around the room and smiled. "She's in excellent company."

"Touché." Dax held up his coffee mug as if he was toasting her. "Right now, I'm leaning toward Donella mixing up the poison. She might have administered it, or it was a group effort. Either way, they all seemed to have a motive to get rid of Petra. Don't forget she wanted to be the big cheese when it came to this paper on Milo's amulet."

Nikki's head whipped around. "What are you talking about, Milo's amulet? Is the Heart of the Soul his?"

I dropped my chin. With the slip of the tongue, Dax blew Milo's cover, which I know Lily had promised him she wouldn't let the secret get out.

Milo leaped into Dax's lap, and with an arched back, he hissed and spit at Dax. I didn't need to be able to understand familiar to know that he was one angry familiar.

"Milo, I'm sorry. I forgot Nikki wasn't a part of the group earlier. I didn't mean to spill the tuna juice."

Milo took a swipe at Dax's face. He wasn't in danger of a scratch as Milo kept his paw far enough away. He jumped down and stalked from the room.

"Will someone fill me in?" Nikki asked Lily. "Also, why didn't you tell me?"

"I'm sorry, Nikki. Milo swore me to secrecy, and I have to stay true to my word always. Even if Milo wasn't my familiar, I'd never share another secret."

Some of the fire in Nikki's eyes dampened. "I know. You're a loyal friend, and I can understand why you wouldn't, but you told these two." She poked a finger in mine and Dax's direction.

"I promise, as soon as Milo were to tell me I could share this with you, I would have." Lily proceeded to summarize yesterday's events after she had left with her Mom. "So, the bottom line is that Milo was mortified that a witch got the upper hand over him. He's hidden that secret for many decades. Now you need to promise that you will never tell another living soul."

She whipped out her wand and held it perpendicular to the floor. It floated in midair as she put her left hand on the wand and her right hand over her heart. "Witches honor I will never share Milo's secret with another living person."

Lily jumped up and threw her arms around Nikki. "Thank you."

Dax stood. "I'll be right back." He hurried down the same row of books where Milo had disappeared.

Lily began to follow him when I put my hand out and touched her arm. "Dax needs to fix this with Milo. Give them a few minutes, okay?"

"Milo never asked for this situation, and if he hadn't been upfront with you, his life's history wouldn't be revealed like this."

I slipped my arm around her waist. "No, he didn't, but how about we talk about the case? My primary suspects are going to want to leave town once the amulet is returned to the exhibit, which means we need to figure out who dun it, and I can't do that without your incredible mind."

She gave me a side-eye. "Are you trying to distract me?"

"Is it working?"

A smile began to creep over her lips. "Maybe." She walked back to her chair and crossed her legs after she sat down. "You can be the scribe."

Nikki looked between us. "Is everything okay now?"

Lily nodded. "It is. Dax can take care of himself with Milo, and to Gage's point, there is a murder to solve, and he can't do it without us. Let's review what we've learned today from Paige and our impromptu conversation with the four suspects."

My brow quirked. "You accidentally ran into Simon, Chaz, Roni, and Donella?"

She winked at Nikki. "It just happened that we were enjoying a cup of coffee and a muffin in the town square earlier today. Minding our own business, you know girl talk and all. When, much to our surprise, Chaz and the ladies came out of the B & B. We know they're staying at the Coastal Motel, and Simon is in town. They stopped to ask us for a recommendation where they could have breakfast."

"Lily. You're playing all innocent with me. Do I need to drag the information out of you? What did you find out? Typically, you're dying to share. And wait, Simon wasn't with them?"

She laughed and clapped her hands together. "I thought you'd never ask." She leaned forward in her chair resting her forearms on her thighs. "It's safe to say these people weren't Petra's friends. Simon wasn't going to get a byline for the article she planned to write with him about the amulet. Effectively, she was going to take all the credit. I get the impression she thought of him as only her assistant even though he was her equal in education and doing the work, maybe more since she probably didn't like getting her hands dirty."

I flashed Lily a look, and she scrunched up her face in response. "I got the distinct impression she bossed him around. So," she drawled out the word, "I took a leap."

Dax rushed back to the seats with Milo. "You guys have to hear this. Milo remembered something."

He jumped from Dax's arms to the empty wingback chair and began to grumble and meow to Lily. "What's he saying?"

"Milo, you're positive?"

He patted her leg with his paw and seemed to nod.

She looked at me. "Milo said they all came out of the library together, and he's pretty sure Petra was taunting them when she said, *you're nothing but a bunch of sore losers.* It was a moment later she cried out, *you idiot, now look at what you've done.* Moments later Milo collapsed.

I studied the board. "Jumping out on a limb, Petra was the person who managed to liberate the amulet from the case. Which led her to call the rest of them losers, and when someone sprayed her in the face, she said the idiot comment. I'll need to bring them back in and question them separately. One of them knows who pushed the pump and sprayed her with the deadly substance."

Milo grumbled again. Lily's shoulder drooped as she said, "We need to examine the amulet. Milo thinks it's possible the combination of the Devil's Hemlock and the curse may have been why she died, and if that's the case, he will surrender himself into your custody."

I dropped to one knee and placed a finger under Milo's chin easing his face up so that he would look at me. "Milo, you need to trust me on this. You are not responsible for the death of Petra Addington, and as far as I'm concerned, you are going to live out my natural life in our," I clasped Lily's hand, "home. We're a family, little man, and don't you forget it."

Out of the corner of my eye, I saw her wipe a tear away. "Dax, we need to head over to the lab. There is an amulet that needs a closer examination, and with your special skills, I need your help."

Giving Lily a quick kiss and a promise I'd call her later,

I looked at Dax. Without a word, he headed for the door, and we left the shop without a backward glance in the direction of the police station. There was no way I was going to let an archeologist and thief come between the love of my life and her familiar. By the stern look on Dax's face, he felt the same way without having to be asked.

Chapter 13
Lily

Nikki and I spent a bit more time at the bookstore, rehashing our conversation with Simon and the crew. However, without talking to them again, there wasn't really anything to go on for the next move. Now as I stood behind the counter stacking invoices into two piles, a thought I had earlier niggled at me. A Michaels witch never caused harm to another; it's how the witches in our family were wired. So how and why would Milo have cursed the amulet in an attempt to cause so many people to come to a nasty end in the moments before he succumbed to being a familiar?

I wandered around the bookstore and checked every one of his hiding places. I needed answers; why would he have wanted to leave a trail of cursed souls just for wearing the amulet? Over the years, innocents could have fallen to dark magic. "Milo, come out from where you're hiding."

The sounds of cat nails clicking against the wood floor drew my attention to the back room, and the kitty door was swinging in the breeze. I slammed my clenched fist into the opposite hand. "Why that little fur ball."

I spun on my heel and went back to the desk. The front door opened, and Simon came in the door, his head down as if the floor in front of him was fascinating.

"Hello, Simon."

He closed the door and came to the desk but avoided actually looking me in the eyes. He wore the same brown suit from the other day. Now it was rumpled, his pale-yellow tie was askew, and the top button of his shirt was undone. At least it seemed he had on a fresh shirt. "Hello. I was hoping you had that book we talked about earlier?"

This was a golden opportunity to see if I could unearth any additional information about the night Petra died. Avoiding his question, I asked, "How are you doing?" Out of the corner of my eye I saw Milo creep along a bookcase in our direction.

He shrugged, his voice flat. "All right, I guess. It's just weird. Petra and I have been a team for a very long time. I know you saw firsthand how she treated me, but she taught me more than any book could have if I had studied for the rest of my life." He lifted his face and he focused his red-rimmed eyes on me. "Do you understand? Chaz, Donella, and Roni don't. They think I should be celebrating that I'm finally out from under her oppressive thumb."

"Simon, I am truly sorry for your loss. It doesn't matter what anyone else thinks about Petra. You're allowed to grieve as you need to. And don't let anyone tell you otherwise."

"Thanks."

Simon Beale was a shell of a man from the first time

he had walked into this store. Was it all a put on? Was his demeanor one of guilt mixed with regret? I reached up and brushed my black tourmaline and amethyst protection necklace. A special gift from Aunt Mimi when I discovered I was a witch. It was cool to the touch, which indicated I wasn't in any danger at the moment. I slipped it under my shirt. Even if he was the killer, within seconds, I could cast a protection bubble around myself.

"Do you know what you're going to do next?"

He cast a glance around the room and leaned closer to me. "Finish what Petra started. I have all her notes. I'm just as qualified as those three bozos who look down their noses at me, thinking I was just Petra's assistant. I have the same post-graduate degree she did. I've worked by her side for years, and I will not let that humiliation she heaped on me be for nothing." A gleam hovered in his eyes. "We'll see who gets to publish the final paper."

Before my eyes, he transformed from the shell of a human being who walked into my store to a man I hadn't seen before. He stood tall and looked at me directly; his thin-lipped smile caused my stomach to clench.

"I hope it all works out for you." That sounded lame, and I needed more from him before he left the store. "Do you think someone meant to harm Petra?"

"After she took off? Yeah. One of them must have followed her and did the deed."

"Can you tell me what happened, from the time you went into the library the night she died?" I heard the hitch in my breath and hoped he wouldn't. This had the potential to be great information.

He narrowed his eyes. "How do you know we went back to the library?"

I certainly couldn't tell him my cat ratted him out. "Someone mentioned seeing the group of you go in the side door."

"Are you going to tell the police if I give you the highlights?"

"You haven't told them all you know?" I crossed my fingers behind my back since, technically, I never answered the question. It wasn't a lie.

"Yeah, I guess they do. I remember seeing you and that detective together, so I figured you guys were tight."

"He's my fiancé. Since you've already talked to him, you have nothing to worry about." Did that sound too much like I was poking a bear? Even with his change in attitude, my necklace was still cool against my skin. I was safe.

He leaned against the counter like he was getting ready for a long story. I didn't care how long he took as long as he spilled his guts.

"It was Petra's idea to go back and take another look at the amulet. Chaz mentioned his friend was the head librarian and she would agree to leave the door unlocked so we could get in. I wasn't thrilled she allowed the others to come with us, but hey, I'm just the assistant. My vote didn't count." His words were laced with the bitterness of a man passed over time and time again.

"Did she plan on stealing the amulet, was that her real motivation to go back?" Out of the corner of my eye, I saw Milo slink around the corner of a bookcase and creep to the counter as if he were stalking prey.

"I don't think so. It wasn't like it would be easy anyway.

The glass isn't glass; it's a super thick and virtually unbreakable plastic, fools almost everyone. Once we got in the annex, I turned the overhead lights on. We discovered there was a hole cut in the front of the case. Petra rushed over so that she could get to it before Chaz, Donella, and Roni. I didn't get the chance to remind her the amulet's cursed. She snatched it from the case and held it up like she achieved a huge victory." He shook his head. "The only saving grace was she didn't put it on. Yet."

"Did the others try to take it away from her?"

He snorted. "Are you kidding? They were all shouting at once, and heck, I have no idea who said what, but it wasn't pretty. Finally, after all the bickering, Petra announced she was leaving and taking the amulet with her. There was a scuffle between the women, but she didn't let go. Somehow, she got the necklace over her head. That's when the chaos ended."

I sucked in a breath, and Milo growled. "She wore it?" I wanted to remind him that she was found with it in her hand but this was his story.

"You should have seen Roni and Donella's face. The color drained while I watched them, watch Petra. I couldn't help but laugh. Who really believes that nonsense about a curse killing anyone who wore it."

I snapped my head in Milo's direction as he sunk his claws into my arm. I had been so intent on Simon's story I failed to see how close he had gotten to me. Easing him off my arm I said, "Then what happened?"

"After they backed off, Petra was ready to get back to our rooms. She told them she hoped there would be no sore losers once she had thoroughly examined the amulet and drafted her paper. She was sure her proposal would clinch a generous offer to do an in-depth article."

"But she didn't go back to the B & B."

"No. This is where things get a little fuzzy. We left as a group, and by the time we reached the sidewalk, Chaz had jostled me, and Petra had been shoved a few times, too. They wanted that amulet in the worst way. Once we were on the sidewalk, Petra was pushed again, and this time, she landed on the ground. She pulled a can of pepper spray from her pocket and held it up, threatening to let them all get a dose if they didn't back off."

"Pepper spray?" Those two words came out in a rush.

"Petra never left home without it. But she dropped it and had to pick it up. Next thing I knew, everyone but me was holding a canister of the stuff, all threatening each other. I don't know who sprayed first but Petra screamed and began to run toward the wharf."

"You didn't follow her?"

"H E double hockey sticks, no. She would never have wanted to appear less than in control in front of me. I knew she'd cool off and come back to her room. Call me on the way and ask for a pot of tea or coffee and be ready to work."

"But Petra never came back, did she? Why didn't you call the police?"

"I fell asleep. It had been a long day, like all days with her. I don't remember what time it was when the police showed up and told me she was dead." The color drained from his face. "Worse moment in my life, ever."

"It wasn't that great for Petra either."

Milo grumbled, "Ask him if she took the amulet off

before everything went down outside of the library. I think I would have remembered if she had been wearing it."

That was a good point. "Do you remember if she was still wearing the amulet?"

He closed his eyes and was quiet for a few minutes. Was he *acting* like he was trying to remember? And when had I gotten so suspicious of people? That was something I needed to talk to Gage about.

"I can't recall. Everything happened so fast once the pepper spray was out and ready to be used." A twitch of the corner of his mouth caught me off guard. What the heck could have been so funny about pepper spray and fighting?

Now he sported a full smirk. "It kinda looked like gunslingers ready for a shootout. You know, pistols out, and who's going to back down first kind of a thing? If things hadn't turned out the way they did, it would have been a comical anecdote down the road."

I got where he was coming from. But it was a bit too soon, given it had only been a couple of days since his boss died. But he was still firmly on my suspect list so nothing would surprise me until the case was solved. "Did you tell Detective Erikson all this information?"

"Except the part about everyone pulling out pepper spray. He knew I was at the B & B from the time I left the library until two officers showed up."

"Did someone confirm what time you came back?"

"Like who? The guy who owns it, Donnie? He checks in with the manager first thing in the morning, and if a guest needs something at night, there's a number to call; otherwise, he's not around."

"Mable Thorpe is the manager."

"Yeah, right. We've met. She's a nice lady, but I get the impression taking care of everything at the inn is a hard job. She didn't even get to doing up my room yesterday."

"Mable is a very nice person." I didn't have any other burning questions, so I said, "Are you still interested in the book on amulets." I withdrew the copy from under the counter and placed it in front of him.

"That's it." Simon pulled out his wallet and handed me some cash for the book. "Thanks a lot for holding on to this for me. I'd hate for one of the happy trio to get their hands on it."

"Simon, one last question if you don't mind." I handed him back his change and slid the book into a small brown paper bag.

"Not at all." He tucked the bag under his arm.

"Do you get along with Chaz, Donella, and Roni, and it's just a professional rivalry?"

"For the most part. Listen, I know Petra was a piece of work, but she was smart, capable, and driven to be the best in our field. I don't think there's anything wrong with that. The others, well they were jealous of Petra. If there was to be a new discovery with the amulet they didn't want it coming from us. Now they're out of luck. I have all the notes I need. Soon they'll realize they were out of their league."

"Will you give Petra a posthumous credit in the byline?"

His brow wrinkled. "Why would I do that? It's not like she'd know the difference, but this will make my career." He tapped his finger on the paper bag. "Thanks again."

As he walked to the door, a piece of paper fluttered to

the floor. He didn't seem to notice. I called out to him but he hurried down the street. I walked across the store and picked it up. It was a receipt from an online store for a six-pack of atomizers. The date was two weeks ago.

I shrieked, and Milo jumped down and trotted over to me. I showed him the slip of paper.

He looked it over. "So, he bought some stuff online. What about it?"

I shook the paper. "Milo, it's a receipt for atomizers. I firmly believe the poison that got on your fur came from one. You didn't get much on you since it drifted from about four or five feet between people, but do you know what this means?"

"That Simon might have gotten free shipping?"

With a deep groan, I said, "No. Simon Beale just moved to the top of the suspect list." I tucked the receipt into my pocket.

Milo crouched and leapt from the floor into my arms. He patted my cheek with his paw. "My dear witch, are you invested in this case just because you found that woman on the beach?"

Hugging him close to my heart I kissed the top of his head. "A small part sure, but the real reason is you. When someone hurts my family, I want to make sure justice is served. Between my skills and Gage, we will find out who almost took you away from me."

I swallowed the sob that threatened to escape my soul. I held him up in front of me and looked into his sage-green eyes. "I do have one question for you, my little fur ball. If you are immortal, how come you almost died?"

Chapter 14
Lily

Milo squirmed out of my arms and dropped to the floor, landing on all four feet. He strutted to the window seat, hopped up, and settled in. There was no way I was letting this little fur ball off the hook from talking to me.

I crossed the room and perched on the edge of the cushion. "Milo, you need to talk to me. I can't help you otherwise."

"I'm not ignoring you. I just don't have an answer as to why the poison affected me." He placed a paw on my hand. "My dear witch, it has me a little worried. There's no indication Petra Addington was a witch, and I feel awful that she died from it. But there is some measure of comfort it wasn't my curse who killed her. And now I've been thinking about all the people this amulet came in contact with, how many innocent people were caught in the crossfire of my battle with one evil witch."

I wasn't going to voice that I had had the same thought. It wouldn't be fair to add to his burden of guilt. "You have no way of knowing what happened after you lost posses-sion of the amulet, so don't berate yourself about what might have happened." As tempted as I was to scoop him up, the way his body was facing the window indicated he didn't want comfort. At least not right now. "I have an idea."

He gave me a kitty side eye roll. "I hope it's a good one."

I scratched under his chin to get him to really look at me. "We could ask Dax if there's a spell or something to check on the curse. Maybe it got diluted over the years, and it's no longer a threat to anyone." Shooting from the hip right now was the only thing I could do. Heck, I didn't even know if it was possible to keep Dax safe while casting a spell to dive into a cursed amulet.

He sat up. "Where's your book?"

I grinned. "Under the counter. Maybe we should go take a look."

As I stood, Milo placed his entire body weight on my hand. "Lily."

Pausing I said, "What's wrong?"

"Whatever the book says, you must make me a promise, and for clarification, a promise between us can never be broken."

"Um, you're starting to worry me."

He kept his body right where it was. "Do you promise me?"

"Don't you think I should know what I'm promising first and do we need to do a blood oath or something?" I was attempting to keep this conversation light as my insides quaked.

He shook his head. "Don't be ridiculous. That's only on

television or in the movies. In the real world, a witch or familiar's word is their bond."

"Good to know on both counts."

He sunk a claw into my hand pricking my skin. "Ouch. You said we didn't need to draw blood."

"You got sidetracked. Will you promise me that no matter what is written in *Practical Beginnings*, you will, under no circumstances, cast a spell to uncover the secrets of the amulet by yourself?"

"Milo, are you worried about me?"

He jumped to the floor, and his tail whipped from left to right and back again. "No. I'm worried you'll mess up the spell and either get yourself zapped by my magic or have it curse me."

I placed my hand over my heart. "Oh, you old fur ball, you're worried about me." I felt a tear prick my lashes.

"Somebody has to; otherwise, you'd just be casting spells willy-nilly." He stalked to the counter and hopped up, casting a glare in my direction. I hurried over.

I placed the book on the counter, and before I opened it, I leaned down to look into my familiar's eyes. "I promise I will not try to examine the amulet without Dax present, and he will do the hard work. I need to know what can be done before I approach him." I kissed the top of his soft fur. "Now, you need to promise me that you will always have my back."

He tipped his head to the side. "I was thinking about that. When you marry Detective Cutie, I think I should be your best familiar."

I couldn't help but smile. "You mean in place of Nikki?"

"Yes. Well, you were her maid of honor so I think in addition to…"

"If you're serious, then you will be an important part of the wedding once we set a date. But first, we need to find out what's going on with your amulet and Petra's death." I placed my hand on the well-worn leather cover of *Practical Beginnings*. "Are you ready?"

He bowed his head as if he was saying a prayer. "We should wait for Dax." He lifted his head. "We're asking him to help us. Even though he won't be able to read the spell on the page as you read it, for practicing he'll need to record it. You'll need to say it together with me present. The power of three."

"We can ask Nikki, Aunt Mimi, Gage's mom, Glinda, and my dad, too, if we need to create a small coven." In a moment like this, I wished I had gotten involved with the local coven. It was on my to-do list, but I wasn't making time for it. I made a mental note to ask Nikki about taking me next month.

"No. I don't want anyone else to know other than who already does. Gage can be with us but that's it." With a sharp bob of his head, I knew there wasn't going to be a discussion or a change of mind on who could be with us when we tried to reveal the secrets of the amulet.

Instead of opening the book, I called Gage and put him on speakerphone. While it rang, Milo stretched his long body over the length of the counter, including covering up my book.

"Hello, sweetheart." Gage's voice was smooth as honey. "Is everything okay?" And there was the concern that tended to seep in when I called him during a case.

"Fine, but I have an idea, and before you say, no, Milo agrees it's something we need to do."

"Alright, I'm listening." His words came out in a slow, thoughtful way.

"Is Dax with you, and can you put me on speaker? He needs to hear this, too, since it involves him."

"He's not, but if you give me ten minutes, we can call you back. Is there something you want to give me a heads-up about?"

"Sure, it involves the amulet, a receipt for atomizers, and Milo."

"I'm intrigued, but I can wait to hear more until I track Dax down."

"Thank you." I ran my hand over Milo, and I could feel the tension in his lean body.

"Lily, be careful okay?" A tinge of worry had crept into Gage's voice.

"Always." I disconnected the call. Milo rolled on his back, paws up. I knew he was looking for a belly scratch, and with all that he had been through, I happily obliged.

"You know Detectives Cutie and Sweet Tea are going to walk through that door instead of calling you back."

"I do." I ran my fingertips over his ribs. "Why are you losing weight?"

"Stress. I can't enjoy my regular meal and special treats you give me when I'm concentrating on other things."

That was odd I hadn't noticed he wasn't eating. His plate was always clean after each meal. "Are you making your food disappear?"

"As in wasting it, no. I can magick it back into the refrigerator when you're not looking. That way, once all this craziness is behind me, I can scarf it down. Including that special smoked salmon you will pick up from Betty's Market when we celebrate." He flipped back to his belly and stretched. "That felt good. Thanks for the mini massage." He dropped to the floor and sauntered into the back room. He paused and looked at me. "Don't worry; I won't be far. I just need some quiet time to think."

I was standing in front of my clue board when Gage and Dax arrived. Just as Milo had said, they showed up instead of calling. Gage quirked a brow when he saw me writing.

He came over and brushed his lips over mine. "Hello, my favorite witch. What's going on here?" He had borrowed one of Milo's terms of endearment without even knowing they shared the same sentiment.

Winking at Dax, I said, "I had a visitor earlier. Simon Beale stopped in and gave me a few tidbits of information and dropped a receipt. Then Milo and I had a long chat, and we've come up with an idea about the amulet, and its history."

Gage perched on the arm of the wingback chair, and Dax remained standing. He seemed to be on high alert as if he knew we might be ready to try something that could be potentially dangerous.

I stepped back from the clue board. "Simon was in to get a book about amulets. While he was here, I discovered a few things about the night Petra died."

Gage opened his mouth, and I tipped my head, "Hold your questions until I share all the details."

He ran his fingers over his lips like a zipper and gave me a nod as if to say I had his full attention.

"As I was saying, Simon said when they got inside the library, the case had already been cut in front of the amulet, and Petra grabbed it before the others could. There was a skirmish, and she ended up putting it on over her head. Of course, there was arguing as well, which continued when they got out to the street. It was then that everyone seemed to have a canister of pepper spray, all fighting to get the necklace. I guess we could say the opal brought out the worst in them all. Petra dropped hers and picked it up, which then resulted in someone spraying her in the face. After that she took off to parts unknown; well, he really said she ran in the direction of the beach. I think we can surmise she wanted to wash her face and the ocean was the closest water source she would have easy access to. We know the rest, she collapsed and that's where she died."

"You think either Chaz or the ladies had, what Petra believed was pepper spray, when it was in fact a deadly substance?" Gage asked

"It makes sense. But let's not discount that it still could have been Simon who sprayed her. We only have his version at this point, but we need to chat with our other three suspects and see what they can confirm. I think it's important they are given some kind of pass for entering the library since Simon and Paige have corroborated the side door was intentionally left open."

Dax crossed his arms and looked at my clue board. "Lily's right, we do need to see what they'll confirm or deny. We need to begin ruling out suspects."

"Paige shouldn't be an active suspect at this point. She

wasn't at the library inside or out. Not that her poor judgment shouldn't be a concern. That should be a topic the town board addresses. Gage, maybe you could recommend she get written up in her file but not fired? Strictly from a detective's point of view?"

He nodded. "That I can do. Now what's next?"

With a glance in the direction of the window seat, which was vacant, I called out, "Milo, can you come over here, please?"

In his best little kitty grumble, he uttered, "Coming."

I waited until he had hopped up on the wingback chair next to Gage before I turned my back to the clue board. "Milo and I talked and we have a few concerns and thoughts about the amulet." I gave Dax a pointed look. "If you don't want to be a part of this, I understand completely but—"

Before I could go any further, he said, "Count me in. I have a feeling you're going down a road where my experience might be useful."

My brow arched.

He shook his head. "Don't get your wand twitching. You've been casting spells for almost a year. I've been working at this my entire life. Talent like yours is important, and experience compliments talent."

Milo was ping-ponging between Dax and I. "Lily, the experienced witch is right. Don't get all weirded out because this needs to be done with the three of us. We know we're more powerful together."

Gage said, "What did Milo say?"

"He's agreeing with Dax that I need to accept his

support due to my lack of experience and that we are stronger together."

Milo hopped off the chair. "Bottom line, Detective, you need to use your skills to cast a spell over the amulet to discover how powerful the magic is. Including if it harmed Petra Addington."

His voice was grave, and I knew this was very difficult for him. "A Michaels witch should do no harm unless it's self-protection. Cursing my amulet was pure and simple revenge, and all because some witch got the upper hand. I lost it. I'm not sure how I can deal with this aftermath."

"Dax, since the amulet belonged to a member of my family I believe we'll find a spell in *Practical Beginnings* that can help us. What I'd like to do is ask the book. It should find what we need. I'll read the spell to you, and if you could record it, that might help us when we cast it."

He nodded. "We'll have to do the spell at the station. But I can create a screen so anyone who comes along won't know what we're really doing."

"Are you sure everyone will be safe?" My gut clenched when I thought of a non-magical person getting caught up in the stars only knew what.

"We'll make sure of it." He held out his hand, and I took it.

Gage stood behind me, his hands on my shoulders. "I'll do whatever you need. But first, I need to see that receipt."

I withdrew it from my pocket and handed it to Gage. "Look. It's dated two weeks ago, and if we look up that product, I'll bet another piece of this puzzle will lock in place. That atomizer was used to dispense the Devil's Hemlock."

He nodded, his face grim. "I'm sure you're right. While you cast the spell, I'll sit quietly at the table and do some research to confirm your theory."

I could feel the color drain from my face and my heart rate ticked up. "Is there a way we can make sure Gage won't get harmed while we cast the spell?"

He said, "Do what you need to, but I'm not leaving you to face this with Dax and Milo as backup. I might not have the skills you need, but I have the most powerful force on my side, love."

My breath caught in my chest, and I leaned into his chest as his arms wrapped around me.

Dax said, "Gage is right. We need him too." He pointed to the book. "We should see what we're facing."

I wasn't sure if this was a smart idea or not, but it had to be done. I patted Gage's clasped hands. "I'm ready."

Chapter 15
Gage

How could I watch the woman I love putting herself on the line to protect another? Especially when there was nothing I could do but stand behind her, offering silent support. Meanwhile, my best friend had the skills to protect her and Milo.

With a flick of Lily's wrist, the CLOSED sign appeared on the door, and the window shades that appeared from nowhere were lowered. Next, we all walked to the counter. Each step I took was slow and deliberate. I was still wrapping my head around why Lily would want to know about the amulet. She couldn't recast a spell to nullify the curse, could she?

Milo hopped onto the counter and sat facing the ancient book. My mom had a similar one, but her book was titled The Beginning; when I was a kid, I wanted to be a witch and tried to read it, but the pages were blank. That was when it was confirmed I was like Dad, non-magical.

Dax asked, "What's your plan?"

Lily tipped her head in my direction and gave me a

reassuring smile. It did little to slow my racing heart. Even if they weren't doing the spell here, this was starting down that path. I tapped my chest and then pointed at her. She placed her hand over her heart and then pointed at me. Who needed words when our hearts were connected?

"When I want to find a specific spell, I close my eyes and place my right hand on the cover. I ask the question and wait for the cover to warm under my hand. When I lift the cover, the pages begin to flip backward and forward, and finally, it settles on the right page. The words are visible to me, and I can read, memorize them, or, in some cases, practice the spell. In this case, I won't be practicing. I'll just read it so we can use it later."

"What specifically are you asking for?" Dax was solely focused on Lily.

She bit her lower lip. "Can we cast a spell over Milo's spell to have the amulet cause no harm?"

Milo hung his head as he meowed.

Dax glanced at Lily. "Milo you know there is no way to discover exactly how many people have worn this necklace. But when we work together, I'm positive we can wrap this amulet in a protective spell that will last for many generations to come. It will never hurt anyone again."

Lily said, "Milo, look at me."

He slowly lifted his head. My heart went out to this tortured familiar. His eyes finally met Lily's.

"You were under attack and did what you had to do to try and protect yourself and the center of your goodness. While under stress you made a poor decision that anyone might have done, including myself. No one is judging you for what happened, and I never will. I'm confident Gage and Dax don't either. It's time you forgive yourself."

Milo took a step toward Lily. He placed his paw on top of her hand as she lay it on the cover of her book of magic. I wished I was a part of this small circle of three, but my place was to wait until I was needed. Lily said to Dax, "Are you ready?"

He tapped his phone. "I'm recording now."

"Long before me, a spell was cast in haste. Now, I want to write a new future of what was done into what will be. Find the spell to guide us three." Her eyes widened as she held her hand in place. Milo meowed to her and withdrew his hand as she smiled. "We've got this."

The moment she lifted her hand from the cover the book flew open with a loud thud against the counter. Briefly, her eyes widened before returning to normal. A small, satisfied smile played over her lips.

The pages had stopped, and the book seemed to be waiting for Lily.

She studied the page.

I wiped my damp palms on my jeans. The clicking of the wall clock grew louder with each passing tick. I wanted to ask what she had found but kept quiet. Magic was an intense process. I didn't want to be the reason the spell didn't work.

"This is interesting." Lily looked from Milo to Dax and then to me. The confidence I saw in her eyes helped me take a deep breath.

"The book is showing me two spells. One to confirm what kind of spell the amulet is bound with, and the other is a protection spell for it to be secured forever."

"Interesting." Dax rubbed his hands together and pointed to the book. "Read the first one. Please."

She cleared her throat. "We need to have the amulet in front of this and then say, *A long time ago, from anger and haste, a spell was cast. Show to me, what now remains from years past. For this I wish so shall it be.*"

"And somehow we'll see something or just know intuitively what has happened?" Dax asked.

Milo meowed, and Lily said, "It doesn't say specifically, so I guess we'll have to wait and see."

Dax stepped closer to the counter, the toes of his shiny black shoes touching the wood. "What is the second spell?"

Why I was focused on the shine of his shoes was beyond me, but at least that felt normal. Every day, Dax came to work with shoes shone, jeans creased, and his shirt starched, his version of a relaxed small-town detective.

"From this day forth, this amulet will be protected by the force of three. Anyone who possesses it will be happy and full of glee. With the power of three, we wish, and so it shall be."

Dax tapped the face of his cell phone. "Read that one again."

She did as he asked. I could see his mouth moving while she was reading the spell again. Milo was focused on Lily. The energy that pulsed around them was palpable. Coming together was the only thing they could do.

When Lily read it one final time, she closed the book and slipped it into her shoulder bag. "We'll take this with us to the station."

I stood. "We should do this now. The power that is

rolling in waves off the three of you is like watching a storm rolling over the Atlantic. I wish I could be a part of it."

Lily crossed the room and slipped her arms around my neck. Looking deep into my eyes, she said, "You are a part of everything. I couldn't do most of what I have done over the last year without your love and support."

I held her tight, knowing I couldn't protect her from what was to transpire over the next few hours. This had to be done, not just for Lily, but for Milo, too. "Are you ready?" I could feel her nod. She stepped from my arms.

"Milo, it's time to go." He jumped down from the counter and trotted to the door. Lily picked up her tote bag and clasped Dax's hand. "In case something goes wonk-a-do, I want you to know that I value your friendship, and you've become the brother I always wanted."

"Lily," his voice cracked, "nothing will go wrong, and I'm honored you consider me a brother and part of your family." He looked at me with a wink. "I guess that means after the wedding, we'll be related too."

I laughed. Thankfully, the tension, which had been wrapped around us like a wet wool blanket, broke. Milo grumbled as he sat next to the front door.

Dax grinned. "We're coming."

Lily picked Milo up and held him close while I opened the door. With a flick of her wrist, it was locked and we were strolling down the brick sidewalk. She said under her breath, "Let's act casually so no one will suspect what we're about to do."

I slipped my arm around her shoulder and said softly. "How would anyone guess you're about to reverse a centuries-old curse."

"Who knows? But I feel like, *witch on a mission, stay clear*, is stamped on my forehead."

"Trust me. I observe people for a living, and you do not exude anything other than walking with your fiancé, cat, and your good friend on a beautiful day."

She hitched up the bag on her shoulder and said, "I'm going to take your word for it."

I ushered Lily and Milo into a conference room in the rear of the building. I specifically chose this room since there was only one window in the door. It would make it easier to camouflage it for any curiosity seekers. Dax had gone to retrieve the amulet out of the locked evidence room.

A light rap on the door jamb drew my attention away from Lily. "Hey Mac, what's going on?"

"Detective, I saw the light on and wondered if you needed something?" He smiled at Lily. "I'm sure you're working on the Addington case."

Getting caught off guard by one of my best officers might have put me in a jam if I hadn't planned for this to happen. "Lily has reason to believe the amulet might have once belonged to a family member, and she asked if she could take a closer look."

Mac's gaze was drawn to the thick book Lily had pulled from her bag. "Something she found in there?"

"Yes. I was reading this book on our family's history, and an illustration caught my eye. It looks so similar to the Heart of the Soul that I asked Gage if I could get a better look at it. The only time I've seen it in person was at the library. Well, except, of course, when we found that poor woman on the beach."

Her shoulders sagged, but she never broke eye contact with Mac. This woman was cool as a cucumber, and it wasn't like she was lying. Well mostly, but she certainly wasn't going to say the amulet had once belonged to her cat.

"That is very interesting. Mind if I take a look at the drawing too? I find family genealogy fascinating."

Dax appeared behind Mac. "Another time perhaps? I don't want to have this out of the evidence room too long."

Mac's brow furrowed. "Oh, yeah sure." He stepped aside so Dax could enter the conference room. "I'll catch you later."

Milo sat at Lily's elbow, and Dax placed the clear box on the table in front of them. Contained inside was the Heart of the Soul amulet. The large red opal had black streaks running through the stone, and it was the size of a quarter. It was absolutely stunning.

"Milo," I asked, "are you sure this was your necklace?"

He tipped his head and yowled at me. I looked to Lily for interpretation.

"He says the necklace is the chain on which the stone is secured and the red opal is the amulet part. He'll give you partial credit on your question."

"Partial credit." I pulled out a chair and sat. "Milo, can you give me some slack? I'm doing my best. I don't have anything like this that I wear."

He gave a pointed look at Lily, who withdrew a necklace from under her top. "Remember, I, too, wear an amulet for protection. If it gets warm, I'm alerted that something is wrong. My aunt wears one as well. Well except when it was stolen in an attempt to frame me for murder."

"I'm glad you wear it. I just never gave it much thought before all this happened."

Dax said, "It's more common than you think. Most people, witches and non-magicals alike wear a piece of jewelry or carry a talisman on their person. They feel it provides them strength or protection. Milo just happened to have a very large and precious stone as his." He affectionately rubbed the top of Milo's head.

I reached my hand into my left pants pocket, withdrew a silver half-dollar, and held it up. "Like this."

Lily's eyes widened as she recognized the coin. "You still have that after all these years?"

I nodded and slid it back into my pocket. "Since the day you left for college and tossed it to me out the car window as you drove away." What I didn't say was that even when we weren't in touch, I always felt she was with me. That's when it clicked; this was my amulet even if it wasn't strung on a strand of gold or silver.

Dax cleared his throat. "If we're ready, let's get started."

Lily pushed back from the table and rose to her feet. The book was on the table in front of her. Milo also stood up, and I made sure the door was closed, and I flipped the lock. There was no way of knowing what might happen, but I had the utmost confidence in Lily and Dax.

Dax extended his hand to Lily and to Milo. They both, in turn, held out their fingers, tip to tip to paw as they formed a circle around the box.

"Lily, are you ready? I want you to say the spell. I will follow your lead."

Her chin trembled, and she rapidly blinked. "I thought you were going to cast the spell?"

He leveled his gaze at her. His voice held that smooth southern drawl that I had heard him use countless times to calm someone down. "I'm not a Michaels witch. However, I will be right here with you. I promise you can do this."

Lily closed her eyes. She exhaled a long, slow breath. When she opened them again, the sable brown eyes were large like dish saucers filled with warmth. She began to speak, her voice held almost a singsong quality I hadn't heard before. "A long time ago, from anger and haste, a spell was cast. Show to me, what now remains from years past. For this I wish so shall it be."

Milo's sole focus was Lily. Rising up from the box that contained the amulet was a brilliant white light. It surrounded Milo as if he glowed with pure radiance. At its base were shades of yellow and green. A sense of calm and peace filled the room, and I had never experienced anything like this before. By the wide-eyed look on Lily's face, she hadn't either. After a few moments, the light was reabsorbed by the opal.

Milo sat back on his haunches.

Lily said, "I'm not sure what that was, but isn't white light a good thing?"

Chapter 16
Lily

As I took a step back from the table, trying to gather my wits about me. I was shocked the amulet didn't show a black light, which would have been very bad. "Milo, do you think this means your amulet isn't cursed?"

He, too, was staring at the box in the middle of the table. "I know I cursed it before I morphed into my current form. Could someone have reversed the spell?"

I looked at Dax. He was the senior witch in the room.

He said, "That's highly unlikely. Whoever came in contact would have to know the exact spell first. As we know, if Milo cursed it and the first witch died, there would be no one to tell after that." He rubbed a hand over the stubble on his chin. "Milo, when you were a witch, what was your main focus?"

"I was more of a generalist like Lily."

"Would you say Lily emulates your ethos?"

He gave a single nod. "Yes. It's also part of the Michaels way. Do no harm."

"By any slim chance do you remember the spell you cast?"

Gage said, "What's going on? Why are you asking about the spell? Is there something we need to be concerned about?"

Dax shook his head. "I have a working theory, but I need some more information."

Milo tipped his head from side to side. He looked at me. "It was such a blur. The crone was waving her wand, cursing me for all eternity and I knew I had to act fast."

He perked up in his stance. If he could have snapped his paws like an ah-ha moment, this would have been it.

"I remember the middle and end of it. *And evil will bounce back on thee, with this curse I wish, so it shall be.*"

Dax sat down at the table. "Milo, are you sure those were your words?"

With a sharp nod, he said, "Yes. I'm sure."

A smile spread on Dax's face, and I knew where he was going with his questions. "Say the words one more time and really listen to what you're saying."

With a slow realization, Milo said, "Lily, I turned the witch's evil back onto her. I didn't cause anyone that was good to die. Ultimately, it was their own darkness." He padded across the table and with his back to me, his kitty voice was barely audible, "I didn't become like her."

I ran my hand down his back. "Milo, all these years you've carried that burden. Do you feel better?"

He bumped my hand with his head. "It will take time to process, but if it wasn't for you, Detective Sweet Tea, and even your Detective Cutie, I would never have discovered the truth. Lily, how can I ever repay you?"

"There is nothing to repay. You're family. We don't keep a balance sheet of who owes what to whom."

Gage cleared his throat. "I got the gist of all that's happened. Milo's amulet was never cursed?"

I pressed my fingers to my lips and took a moment before I said, "He cast a spell to force whatever evil was going to be used to be like a mirror and ricochet back. If a death resulted from trying to use Milo's amulet, it wasn't his doing. It was the caster of the actual spell at that moment. Effectively, he protected what was good and pure."

"Now that we know the amulet is safe, do you still need to do the new spell?"

Dax said, "We should. Since the amulet won't reside with the coven and, as we all know, the Michaels are very powerful witches, we wouldn't want this used for any nefarious reasons in the future."

"Making this extra step is the prudent thing to do." I scooped up Milo. "What do you say, fur ball? Are you ready to use your magic one more time today?"

He tapped his paw on my chin. "My dear witch, it would be my honor to cast this spell with you. But for the record, we're not going to make this a habit, you and me casting together. Well, except we could go fishing and cast. I'd be down for that."

I couldn't help but chuckle. Leave it to Milo to put food back into the equation. "I'm sure that can be arranged." I set him in the same place he was for the first spell. Dax stood, and we once again created a link between the three of us. "Are we going to repeat the protection spell three times?"

Dax nodded. "Yes, and like before, you'll begin, and Milo and I will join you."

I closed my eyes and thought of the words I was about to say. The link between the three of us was strong and comforting at the same time. I was ready. "From this day forth, this amulet will be protected by the force of three. Anyone who possesses it will be happy and full of glee. With the power of three, as we wish, so it will be."

As before, we repeated it two more times. At the conclusion, I opened my eyes and looked at the amulet lying in the circle. I wasn't sure if it was a trick of light, but I could have sworn the center of the opal glowed. I glanced at Milo. He gave me that slow, saucy kitty wink that confirmed he had seen it too.

"Now what do we do?" I looked around at Gage and Dax.

Dax picked up the container. "Put this back into evidence, and Gage and I will get to work and solve Dr. Addington's murder."

"About that." I gave Gage a firm look. "You need to look at that chemistry of the poison. Who had access to the ingredients to make it and the opportunity? Even the cylinder that was used to dispense it, did Simon make the purchase, or was it a coincidence he had the receipt?"

Gage slipped an arm around my waist and steered me toward the lobby. "Lily, I know you're dying to get your wand into my case. I promise Dax and I have several promising leads. But if I have any questions, I'll be sure to run them past you." He kissed my cheek and opened the door.

Milo trotted down the wide stone steps and called out

to me, "See you at the bookstore. I'm going to see a few friends."

There was a jauntiness to his trot that hadn't been evident for the last several days. "Look at him." I pointed to Milo's retreating form. "The weight of the universe has been lifted from his soul."

"He's carried the burden of the belief that he potentially harmed innocent and not-so-innocent people. To understand if something bad happened it was a direct result of someone with cruel intentions has to be a relief."

I leaned into Gage and rested my head against his shoulder. "At least one part of this mystery was solved."

He gave me a reassuring squeeze. "And I will solve the murder. You can sell some books or read your book of *Practical Beginnings*."

I gave him my best evil-eye look. "Again, with the read the book?" I placed my hand over the flap on my shoulder bag as if I needed reassurance that my book was still in there. "Are you sure you're not able to converse with Milo? That's his comment on repeat." That's when I realized he hadn't badgered me since Petra walked into my bookstore. This whole amulet thing had shaken Milo to his core. I'd best be ready now for him to start prodding me to practice my spells. "What do you want to do for dinner?"

He chuckled softly. "Having dinner at your place with the gang so we can talk about the case?"

I couldn't help but grin. This man knew me so well. "Let's barbeque, and I'll text everyone. Since we're not talking curse anymore, I'll be sure to include Mac and Sharon, too." Standing on my tiptoes, I brushed my lips over his. "I might need you to swing by the market on your way over, but I'll let you know."

Dax strolled around the corner. "What are you up to?"

Gage said, "Dinner at Lily's. We're going over the case. And before you say anything, I've already told her we had it under control. But we both know keeping this conversation active is the best way to keep her out of mischief."

"What do you want me to bring and what time?" His gaze was drawn to the town square across Doenut Drive which was directly in front of the police station.

Curious I turned my attention in the same direction. Chaz, Donella, and Roni were sitting on a bench close to Walter's bakery. I suddenly had a craving for coffee.

"Come any time after five and just bring yourself." I slipped from Gage's half embrace and said, "Gotta run. Coffee and then get the store reopened."

Before Gage and Dax could utter a syllable, I dashed across the street and hurried over the grass. Coffee could wait, this was a golden opportunity I wasn't about to pass up.

"Hello there." I waved to the trio as I made a beeline in their direction. My mind raced with how to start the conversation, confident it would come to me, I didn't slow my feet.

The conversation died as I reached them.

Roni said, "Hi." Her green, cat-like eyes narrowed. This was the first time I had noticed them.

My smile included each of them as I looked from Roni to Chaz and then to Donella. "How are you doing?"

Roni said, "Fine. We're just talking about our proposal regarding the amulet."

"That's exciting. Have you spoken with Simon?"

Chaz's smile faded. "Why would we?"

Did they not know he also planned to submit a proposal to become the expert on Heart of the Soul? If they didn't, I wasn't about to break the news to them. However, I needed to take this opportunity to discover who knew the most about the poison that killed Petra.

"I just figured with you all in the same field and him having Petra's notes, it might be beneficial to work together, you know since he has good information."

Donella gave a snort. "Her research is nothing special. She should have stuck to chemistry, which was where she excelled. Of course, not quite as good as Roni, but a close second."

I liked where this conversation was heading. "Is chemistry a valuable skill in archeology?"

She shrugged. "It can be. That's why we all have concentrations in several subjects, like statistics and history too."

"I heard that you all had quite the argument with Petra after she took the amulet."

I saw Roni's eyes briefly widen with surprise before they returned to her normal cool stare. "Petra flaunted that she had possession of it, and her plan was to take it back to her room, do an in-depth study, and return it to the library before the sun came up. But she screwed that up, dying on the beach with the amulet in her hand."

With an empathic nod, I just listened, hoping she'd keep spewing her anger.

"If only she hadn't pulled pepper spray on us. Why she had to think we would try and take it from her at that point was just nuts. There is no way any of us, or Simon for that matter, would have tried to rip it from her hand. That could have damaged the artifact. As lovers of history, we value objects for their beauty and mystery. So, before you ask, when she pulled her canister out, we all reacted the same way. It wasn't right, but she was completely out of line."

"Did you tell the police what happened?" Gage needed to get his hands on their cans of pepper spray to see whose contained what substance.

"It wasn't relevant," Roni's tone was razor-sharp.

How was I going to find out which one of these people understood Devil's Hemlock? "Do you always carry your pepper spray with you? I mean, this is a small town, and you were together as a group." Dang that sounded lame.

Chaz smirked. "Bad things can happen anywhere. Just ask Petra. Oh wait, you can't. She's toes up."

My mouth dropped open, and I took a hasty step back.

Donella whirled around to face Chaz. "Really? Have a little respect for our former friend."

Not wanting to assume they were saying she was former due to the competitive work they were doing or her death, I let that comment slide. "You know there is one thing that bothers me?"

Now focused on me, Donella said, "You're a nosy one, aren't you?"

With a shrug and a small smile, I said, "Curious is more like it."

"What do you want to know?" Chaz asked.

"Simon mentioned the case was cut when you arrived that night. Which one of you has the tools to cut glazing?"

They looked between the three of them. Chaz pursed his lips, Roni blinked rapidly, and Donella said, "Who did cut the glass?"

I had to wonder if they would use glass and plastic interchangeably or if they knew the truth and were deliberately holding back what the material really was.

Chaz ran his hand over his chin. "It had to have been Simon or Petra. We've never done anything like this before. I mean, I fully expected to take some pictures through the case and try to get as close as possible, but the fact that Petra was able to put her hands on the amulet was a shock. I guess that's why it never really registered with us, you know, about the glass being cut when we got there."

Was he to be believed, or could this be a smoke screen for my benefit? It was possible the three of them had a hand in successfully getting Petra out of the way. But the only way to prove that was to find out which of them still had a canister with pepper spray or whether they all contained Devil's Hemlock.

I glanced over my shoulder to where I had left Gage and Dax. They were still on the steps of the police station. "A bit of unsolicited advice. You might want to give the police a new statement about the display case being cut before you arrived at the library. In addition, give them permission to look in your motel rooms before you go back. This way they can eliminate you as a formal suspect." I didn't bother to clarify if I was talking about cutting the display case or Petra's death. Investigating other murders that had happened around town, it was only when the murderer was cornered that they lashed out. If Chaz, Roni, and Donella thought they were in the clear, they'd gladly let Gage and Dax take a look around.

A slow smile appeared on Roni's lips. "That is a very good idea. But one of us didn't kill her. Petra was killed by the curse."

Donella rolled her eyes. "Not too bad for a mere book-shop owner."

I didn't like the swipe at my intelligence, but I was convinced this would help the investigation. At the end of today, I hoped we could have a firm suspect in custody.

Donella glanced in the direction of the police station. "If you're done with your insinuations about us we'll just check in with those hunky detectives before we leave town."

"And I have several things to do as well." I gave a brisk nod at them and whirled around on my heel headed in the direction of the B & B. Before anyone was going anywhere, I needed to find the tool that was used to cut the case, and I was starting with Petra's room and then Simon's.

Chapter 17
Lily

Nikki was waiting for me at the B & B as I hurried up the front steps. "How did you get here before me?"

She held up a bakery box. "I had to drop off scones and muffins for breakfast tomorrow, and I was already on my way."

I pulled open the door, and we entered the tomb-like inn. Ever since Saint Patrick's Day, the B & B had a different vibe and not one I relished. After all, I had come too close to haunting the place in ghost form.

"Do you want to poke around in a couple of the guest rooms?"

I looked around to see if we were alone before I said, "Yes. In talking with our three visitors, they say the glass was cut when they arrived at the library after it was closed. Someone had to have gone over early to have cut it, and my guess is it was Simon. He could have done it at Petra's request or because he planned on taking it for himself. My guess is he did what he was told."

"He doesn't seem like the type to take initiative."

I withdrew my phone. "Before we go upstairs, I'm going to text Gage and let him know to expect company."

Nikki quirked a brow.

"Chaz, Roni, and Donella were going over to let him know they want to leave town. I suggested they offer to have their rooms searched before they pack up. It seems it's common for a person to have a minor in chemistry and history to become an archeologist. I still think one of them is hiding something about that poison. But they're all capable of creating it."

At the B & B. Going to take a quick look around. See you later. Xo

The text was sent, and I put the phone on silent before I slid it into my back pocket. Moving slowly into the room, placing each step with care to create as little noise as possible Nikki followed me. I paused in the main lobby as she placed the box of pastries on the desk. I pointed to the stairs, and she nodded.

Keeping the soles of our shoes in the center of the tread squarely on the carpet we crept our way to the second floor. I whispered. "A guess which room Simon is in?"

She looked up and down the hall and pointed to the door next to the room that had yellow crime scene tape across it. "She'd have him next door to keep tabs on him, and if she wanted to work, he'd be handy. A win-win for her."

I gave her a thumbs-up and moved in the direction of Petra's room. It was easy enough to unlock the door and look inside from the hallway without disturbing the barrier Gage had erected. The next door down opened with a thud.

Simon stepped into the hall with a scowl on his face. His pale blue shirt was untucked, his hair was sticking out in uncontrolled spiral curls, and his face was in desperate need of a shave. "What are you doing here?"

The direct approach was always the best when I had Nikki by my side. "I wanted to look in Petra's room."

"Why?" The question was more demanding than curious.

"We need to discover who cut the display case. Whoever did must have the equipment close at hand."

"I can tell you who did, and it will save you the bother of looking in Petra's room. It was Roni. That woman will do just about anything to get her hands on whatever she believes she's entitled to." He rubbed his hands over the scruff on his chin. "The only thing I can't figure out is why she didn't just take the amulet when she had the chance?"

"For the drama of taking it in front of Petra?" Nikki said. "Poke the bear so to speak."

He thrust his chin up, and a glint came into his eye. This was the second time I had seen he had a backbone.

"Yeah that would have really ticked Petra off, but she got to it first. That plan backfired."

I thought of the comment that Roni made about Petra's cause of death. Could Simon hold the same belief. "Have the police released a cause of death to you?"

Taking a step closer to me, he dropped his voice as his face was devoid of any emotion. "It was the curse."

Could he seriously believe in the curse too? One of the

people at the library that night knew it wasn't a curse but human intervention that caused her death. "You're a believer?"

He stared at me. His voice quivered, "You don't?"

"No. I think it was a live person who caused her death."

He stumbled back, his hand grasping the door jamb as his face drained of color. "That would mean that someone at the library killed her."

Nikki and I each took an arm and maneuvered him into his room guiding him to a chair. Nikki stepped into the adjoining bathroom. I could hear the water running, and she came back with a full glass.

"Sip slowly."

His eyes were fixed on the window, and he did as he was told. Taking a gulp, he muttered, "Murdered?"

Nikki bobbed her head in the direction of a neatly arranged stack of boxes and books next to the bed. Peeking out from under the bed skirt was a long metal measuring stick. There was some kind of a wheel attached and a suction cup at the opposite end. I wanted to wrap my arms around her in a bear hug. That was a glass cutter, and it was large enough to have cut the hole to liberate the amulet. Bingo. Gage needed to get over here. My fingers itched to send him a text, but I didn't want to leave the room. If Simon knew what we had discovered, there was no telling what could happen. However, the summoning spell was the perfect solution.

I stepped back from Simon. Now I was directly behind him. I closed my eyes and silently cast my spell. *Gage, please come to me. There is something you need to see. For this I wish, so it shall be.*

Nikki smiled. She knew our backup was on the way, and for once, I wasn't being held at gunpoint, being threatened with a knife, or with a bottle of poison.

"Lily?" Gage's voice reached us as we were watching Simon drink water. He continued to stare out the window. It was odd the shock of learning it wasn't a curse that killed Petra had caused him this much distress. It left him basically incapable of moving. Did guilt cause a person to freeze up like this?

I stepped into the hall while keeping an eye on Simon in case he made a lightning-fast move to harm Nikki. "Up here."

Gage came around the top of the stairs, and relief washed away the worry lines on his face. He rushed to me. "Are you okay?"

"Yes. Nikki and I are fine, but we discovered something that you need to see." I took his hand and pulled him into the room.

"What's wrong with Simon?"

I shrugged. "Shock? I said I didn't believe a curse killed Petra, that she died because of a real person, and he devolved into this."

"Interesting." He walked deeper into the room. "Simon, are you okay with me taking a look around?"

He nodded. "Sure. Feel free to look in the boxes. There is a great deal of research on the Heart of the Soul." He looked at me, his face drawn. "I swear it's cursed. It says so in all the books. That's why Petra was determined to get her hands on it."

My eyes narrowed. "Did she want to control the purported curse?"

He shook his head. "Just the opposite. She discovered a counter-curse and felt if given the opportunity, she could change the course of history. Not just with the Heart of the Soul but with other artifacts as well. You wouldn't believe how many times we've encountered items that carry darkness from the past. Petra had a mission to change our tiny slice of the world." He hung his head as if sharing this information had been a heavy burden to carry any longer.

Gage's eyebrow arched. I gave him the look that I knew he needed to know what I knew. That was a convoluted thought which made me smile.

I pointed to the floor next to the bed. "Under the bed skirt. There looks to be a glass cutting tool."

His eyes widened. "Have you touched it?"

"Nope." I pulled out a pair of latex gloves from my shoulder bag and passed them to him. "Just in case you don't have a pair." Then I flicked open a jumbo-size zip-top plastic baggie and handed that to him as well.

He grinned. "Is this a new thing for you, Lily? Gloves and pseudo-evidence bags?"

"Being prepared is starting to come in handy." I pulled the bag back. "But if you have your own that's fine too."

With a laugh, he tugged it from my hands and pulled the gloves on with a snap. "Simon, just to be crystal clear, you have given me permission to look around in my official capacity as a detective?"

"How many times do I need to say yes." His response was short and downright rude. As if talking to Gage was interrupting him as he was doing critical work.

Kneeling next to the bed, Gage folded the bed skirt over the mattress. I had my phone ready to take pictures. He looked closer and then rocked back on his heels.

"Simon, is this yours?"

"Is what mine?" He looked up, first at Nikki, then me, and finally at Gage.

"This tool." Gage pointed to it but hadn't brought it out into the open.

"No. I've never seen it before. What is it?"

He either didn't know or knew and was going with plausible deniability.

Gage said, "A tool to cut glass."

Simon chuckled. "You can't cut a circle into a glass case with that. It's not like Hollywood. Where you score the circle and then pop it out. You need access to both sides to tap it out."

He stood up. Gage quickly rose to his feet and rested his hand on his waist, his sidearm within inches of his fingers.

"You seem to know a bit about glass cutting. Would you care to go over to the police station with me? We can sort out ownership of this particular object?"

"Just check for fingerprints. I've never touched that in my life." He looked at me. "Come on, someone has to believe me."

Gage said, "I never said I didn't believe you, but it is in your room. Under your bed." Gage put extra emphasis on the word, *is*.

"If I were in your shoes I'd probably think the same thing." His shoulders slumped. "Guess I won't be leaving town tonight."

"Would you step into the hall, Simon?" Gage ushered him out. "I need to call for someone else to come and bag the cutting tool for evidence."

"Gage, we can wait for Sharon and Mac if you want to go on over."

"Lily," I could see the corner of his mouth twitch as he tried to suppress a grin. Gage knew exactly what I was up to. Once they were gone Nikki and I could poke around more to see what else I might find.

"I don't think so. Peabody and Mac will need to do a thorough search of the room and collect any other evidence they might find. I can have someone run the prints on the tool once they get it back to the station. All of that needs to be done by professional law enforcement officers, not amateur sleuths, even if they do think they're the female versions of Sherlock Holmes and Dr. Watson."

"Fun stealer." I scuffed the toe of my shoe on the rug. It didn't matter that he was right. If there was additional evidence to be gathered, it needed to follow the chain of custody of evidence. "Can we hang around and watch?"

He shook his head. "You're incorrigible. And on the condition of a promise. Since I know if I say no, you'll find a way to get into other mischief."

I crossed my fingers behind my back. Just in case I needed to fib a tiny bit. "What is it?"

"When you leave the B & B, you promise not to make any additional stops," of which he put air quotes around stops, "and I'll see you later at your place."

That was something I could live with, at least until I saw what Sharon or Mac might find. "Sounds like a plan."

Simon said, "No one will mess up my research, right?"

"Everything will look pretty much the same when you get back as it does now," Gage said.

The front door banged, and a moment later I could hear someone running up the stairs. Dax appeared at the top. He looked left and then right and said, "I thought I'd swing by here just in case I can lend a hand."

Gage said, "Perfect timing. I want to get Simon to the station for a statement, and we're waiting for Peabody and Mac to arrive. Would you care to keep the ladies company while they wait?'

This was code for keeping us out of trouble.

"I can take Mr. Beale if you'd prefer to stay, Detective Erikson."

Gage was already escorting Simon down the hall. "Thanks, but I've got this. Lily can fill you in."

He gave me a pointed look when he paused at the top of the stairs. "Remember your promise."

"I will. Don't worry. Dax is here." I still had my fingers crossed behind my back. Dax stepped behind me. I could hear him chuckle softly.

Gage shook his head. "Good luck, Dax, they're all yours."

The moment he was out of sight I whirled around. "We need to get into Petra's room before Sharon gets here. Care to assist or turn a blind eye?"

He leveled his gaze at me. "Was that part of the promise you just made to your fiancé?"

"No. I said I would leave here and head home when I was done."

He turned me around and saw my fingers weren't

crossed. "Okay, we can take a fast look from the hall. But we're not going in. We need to protect any evidence."

"I know the drill." With a grin, I said, "Things aren't going to be the same when you start working in Robin's Pointe. I'm going to miss this."

With a chuckle, he said, "If you tell Gage this, I'll deny it. But I'm going to miss our little adventures too." With a wave of his hand, Petra's guest room door opened.

In two quick steps, toes on the threshold I was leaning into the room and taking pictures as fast as my phone could click.

Chapter 18
Gage

I walked with Simon to the police station unsure if he would start talking about the case or remain silent. It was a surprise when out of the blue he began to talk about stained glass.

"Lately I've started to make small pieces of stained glass. Just look up there." He pointed to the window above the church entrance. "That is a beautiful example of an artisan's work."

With a sharp glance in his direction, I found this information curious. "How long have you been doing that?"

"Petra gave me a couple of classes at a studio for my birthday two years ago. I found it allowed my creative side to grow. I've always loved to draw. Sketching objects so she could take them home was always one of my contributions when we were working. They're better than digital pictures. If there is, or was, something she wants, wanted, to get a closer look at, she'd ask me to focus on it and really pull out the fine details."

"Do you have a studio you work out of?"

Simon sighed. "I set up a bench in my garage. Well, it's less of a garage now and more like a full-fledged studio. Petra was teasing me right before we came to Maine. She stopped by to check out the window insert I was making for her stairwell. You know where you go up halfway to a landing?"

I nodded. Waiting for him to continue.

"She loves, loved, peonies. The season is fleeting as those flowers bloom in late May or early June. As a thank you for getting me started, I offered to create a pane for that window when she remodeled her house. The wood trim is a rich walnut, and this is going to look stunning."

Without bothering to correct him that it wasn't going to be necessary now, I said, "Did Petra stop by your studio often?"

"Once every couple of months. She wanted to keep track of the design and timing of the project, and of course, she wanted to select the perfect peony colors."

He didn't say the words that she was a person who liked control. That had been obvious the one time I had seen her in action at the library. "I've never seen anyone make stained glass. Do you work with pieces of glass that are precut?"

"Other than purchasing single sheets, and some of them are a rainbow of colors, no, I have a grinding stone, but mostly I use hand tools."

We walked up the steps to the station. I held open the heavy glass and wood door. Inside, the sounds of phones ringing, conversations humming, a copier running, and the thunk of a drink can dropping in the vending machine greeted us. I acknowledge Officer Shepard who was covering the front desk. Giving him a nod in greeting I said, "I'm going into conference room one."

It was normally referred to as interrogation room one, but I didn't want to get Simon's guard up as I needed for him to continue to be chatting.

"Would you like a coffee, water, or soda?"

"A ginger ale, if you don't mind. My stomach is a bit upset from all the stress."

Shepard said, "I'll bring it in, Detective. Do you want a coffee?"

"Please." I ushered Simon inside the room and noticed the green light on the camera was steady. "Take a seat." I pulled out a chair on the side of the rectangular table and waited for him to sit down.

Simon looked around the room. There were posters for the Heimlich maneuver and CPR; otherwise, the room was basic: tan walls, a nondescript oak wooden table, and four matching chairs.

Simon said, "The place could use some color."

"It serves the purpose. Why don't you tell me a little more about when Petra stopped by your studio."

He tapped and steepled his fingertips, waiting for my next question. The door opened. Shepard came in with a bottle of ginger ale and a to-go cup of coffee for me.

"Anything else Detective?"

I took the coffee, and Shepard handed the ginger ale to Simon.

"Why don't you stay? I think you told me once that you admired stained glass. It seems Simon knows how to make it and was sharing his process." It was a bit of a stretch, but I hoped Shepard would understand about different tools.

He caught my eye and slowly blinked one time as he pulled a chair from under the table. He got the message. "I'd be fascinated to learn more. I collect it but don't have a creative bone in my body to make it." He chuckled. "My wife says if I bring in one more piece, I'll need to add an addition to the house to have a place to install it all."

The corners of Simon's lips tipped up. "I hear what you're saying. I started off with a small area in my garage. Now my car sits in the driveway. I probably should think of adding on a dedicated workshop." With a shrug of his shoulder, he stopped talking, twisted the cap off the soda bottle, and took a tentative sip. "Thanks, this hits the spot."

"You're welcome," Shepard said. "How did you get interested in making stained glass? I've always been in awe of anyone who can do it."

"In my line of work, we're tasked, at various times, to examine stained glass. If an artifact is discovered, especially if it's intact, which is rare, it can happen. Petra, Dr. Addington would offer up me to do the work. She gave me a lesson pack with a true artisan as a birthday gift." He clasped his hands in front of him and dropped his head. "I know the woman everyone thought she was, but to me, she was tough but also kind. I'm not sure that makes sense."

"The work persona and the personal?" I asked.

He nodded. "Yeah. She took an active interest in my hobbies." His sad smile reinforced my suspicion, they had a strong bond.

"When I showed her my next project, after hers, of a lighthouse she said she was looking forward to seeing the finished piece. That's when she suggested since we were coming here, I might be able to draw inspiration from our visit. We had plans to go out to the lighthouse before we left."

"Did you bring any of your tools with you to work here?"

Simon glanced up and, with a strained laugh, said, "No. It's not a knitting bag you can toss in the back seat. I work with glass. It breaks."

"Detective," Shepard said, "Simon probably uses a grinder and cutting equipment that isn't portable either."

"Oh, the cutters are small with suction cups to attach securely to glass. I wouldn't need to bring them with me."

I stood and excused myself for a moment from the room. Once in the hall, I dialed Peabody. I needed for her to look for a second glass cutter. One of them had to cut the display case, and my money was on Simon. The why? My gut was telling me he'd do almost anything for Petra.

"Hey, Detective."

"Peabody, I need for you to look for another glass cutter in Simon's room. There's one under the bed, and if there is a second, I'm not sure how big it would be. It should have a suction cup on one end, and the other side should have some knife to score glass. If you find something like this, text me a picture. If you find it in Petra's room, label it with an A, and Simon's a B."

"We've already cleared Simon's room and found only the one box. Nothing else remotely resembled your description. He has a stash of books and journals, a laptop, and a notebook with handwritten notes. We just started in Petra's room, but this is the second time we're going through it. We searched it after we found her."

"Do they have in-room safes at the B & B?"

She didn't speak right away. "I'm not sure. Let me see if Mac knows. I've never seen one. Also, I'll check with Donnie and get back to you."

"Thanks." I stashed my cell in my pocket and returned to Shepard and Simon. The conversation was on cutting techniques.

Taking a seat across from Shepard. "Simon, you're saying that not all glass," which I did air quotes around the word glass, "is really glass?"

"No. There are some amazing plastic sheets that have the clarity of glass but are much stronger, so they don't break. Think of jewelry store cases. Typically, everyone thinks they're glass. But in high crime areas, cases have been switched to an acrylic product, with additives, to increase its break resistance. The average person would never know it's not glass."

"Could you use those for creating stained glass work?" Shepard asked.

"Why bother? In stained glass we use lead. It's lightweight and keeps its shape, supporting the glass. But interestingly, many display cases that are used for traveling exhibits are made from plastics. They're half the weight of glass and protect the exhibits without worrying about breakage."

I locked my gaze on Simon as I sat up straight in my chair. "Were they used in the display for this amulet exhibit?"

"Most likely. To be honest, I didn't bother to check. The way the artifacts and amulets had been placed, it was easy to see from all angles, the lighting was excellent. I was able to gather the information I needed."

"Can you cut plastic the same way you do glass and with the same tools?"

Simon finally looked at me. I'm not sure if it was the gravity of the questions now rolling off my tongue or if he knew something specific. Like he was the only one capable of cutting the glass. He had the tools, the know-how, and the opportunity.

"I would assume it's similar, but I've never tried. Detective Erikson, are you accusing me of cutting the display case to gain access to the amulet?"

"Are you about to confess to committing the crime?"

Simon folded his arms over his chest. My text pinged with an incoming message. I said, "Hold on one moment; this could be important."

I studied the picture before turning it around. "Simon, is this your glass-cutting equipment?"

His eyes widened, and his mouth gaped open. "What the..." He looked at me. "You know it's mine since it has my initials on the handle. Petra gave it to me as a gift."

"She sure did give you a lot of gifts. In return did you agree to cut open the display case so she could steal the amulet?"

"No!" He shoved his chair, it bounced off the wall behind him, rebounding to return to its original spot. "I might be Petra's lackey, but I would never, not for her or anyone, commit a crime. I'm a scientist of history. I would never condone theft, and on that I'd stake my life and reputation."

"With Petra out of the way, you have an opportunity to make a name for yourself, isn't that correct?"

"Yes, but I wouldn't steal to gain the limelight. I'm not

an egomaniac out to win at all costs. Besides I was confident the proposal Petra and I would submit would be strong enough to be awarded the opportunity to examine the Heart of the Soul. It would be the highlight of both our careers to date."

"Maybe you realized your solo career would take off and doors would open for you if you made a bold move. That's why you did it."

He pounded the table. I jumped back in the chair. Up to this point, Simon had exhibited beta tendencies.

"I did not cut a hole in that case."

I was done tiptoeing around this conversation. "Then who did?" My words might have come out with more force than I had intended, but Simon didn't shrink from me. Finally, I was getting somewhere.

He stuttered, "I, I can't... I can't say."

"Can't or won't?"

He glared at me. Beads of sweat popped along his upper lip as his face reddened. "I don't appreciate the insinuation."

"Talk to me. Tell me what happened so that I can help you." My cell pinged. I wanted to look at the text, but it felt like I was making headway with Simon. To break the tension would be unwise.

He pointed to my phone. "Aren't you going to get that? It might be important."

"You have officers searching the B & B." He folded his arms across his chest and leaned back in the chair with his eyes closed. "I'm not going anywhere." He opened one eye and said, "Innocent men don't run."

I turned the phone over and looked at the image. This

time, there was an open box with a beaker, mortar and pestle, two baggies of what looked to be dried herbs, and several atomizers that looked exactly like the one we had found that contained the Devil's Hemlock. Another image pinged in: heavy-duty chemist gloves and a package of face-masks. The caption read: Simon's room for protective equipment and Petra's for the poison supplies.

Holding the phone up so that Simon could see the images as I scrolled, I watched him with each image. His eyebrows squished together as he ran a hand over his head. "What is all this?"

"We found supplies in Petra's room to blend a poison and in your room the protective equipment." I stood up. "Simon Beale, I'm placing you under arrest for the theft of the Heart and Soul amulet and for the murder of Petra Addington."

"But I didn't do either of those things. I promise." He placed his hands flat on the table. "Please sit down. I'll tell you everything. I swear it will be the full truth. Once I tell you what happened, you'll know I couldn't possibly have done either of those things. I loved Petra; there was no way I'd ever hurt her.

I sat down. "Go ahead. I'm listening." My cell pinged again. This time, I ignored it. It kept pinging. I took a quick look. The image of another canister next to the back of a spare pillow was in full color. What the heck was going on?

Chapter 19
Lily

Milo was perched on the top step as I came out of the B & B door. Nikki walked next to me. "Are you going to tell me what you discovered?" she asked.

I glanced over my shoulder to make sure we were alone. "When we get back to the bookstore." I scooped Milo up and jogged down the steps. On the short walk back to the store I thought of the room like a movie set. Even though I had taken a ton of pictures, there was a troubling vibe that permeated the space. It wasn't magical but still oppressive. Had Petra been dabbling in something she shouldn't? It didn't hold the same energy when we were in Simon's room. But could it be I was picking up on what had happened there over Saint Patrick's Day and the murder of poor John Bailey? Or could Petra's room have been the point of plotting to steal the amulet by the both of them? One thing I knew for certain, I had too many questions and not enough clarity to see the answer that must be sitting right in front of me.

Sliding my fingers from right to left in front of the door I heard the lock spring free, and the door eased opened. There were little conveniences that I really enjoyed about being a witch. I wondered what else I would find *normal* in a few more months or even years.

We strode in, and I placed Milo on the window cushion so he could snooze in the sun.

"My dear witch, is there a reason why you think I want to be out of the loop on this investigation?" Milo thumped to the floor, stalked to a wingback chair, and hopped up. My familiar turned around three times and then sat down on the chair Gage typically occupied. "I'm ready to review the details and solve the crime of who tried to kill me and why?"

"Milo, we know you weren't the intended target. You came so close to dying even with your claim of immortality." I hurried across the room and picked up my book, Practical Beginnings.

"What do you mean, my claim? I've been alive for generations of Michaels witches, and you're just one in a very long line."

I heard the snark in his tone. Even though I had trod on the line of his feelings, I needed to be logical. What was it about that particular poison that brought him so close to death, and why had someone chosen those particular plants? Hemlock alone was enough to cause respiratory failure. Combine that with the abnormal heart rate of Devil's Snare and psychosis before death, that was a very potent poison.

"Look, Milo, I'm not trying to be unkind. I've researched the two plants that were used in the poison. A small amount in a concentrated form of one plant would have been enough to take a life. With the two combined and depending on the concentration, it could have been more than enough to overtake your system instantly. Heck, we know it almost did. If it hadn't been for Aunt Mimi's quick thinking and skill, I would have lost you."

He dropped his head. "This means I'm down to eight lives."

I sank to my knees in front of the chair and tipped his chin up so I could see his handsome little face. "I only have one life so we'll spend it together." I kissed the tip of his pink nose. "As long as that's okay with you."

Milo tipped his head to the side and looked deep into my eyes. "I guess that will work for me." He gently tapped my cheek with his paw. "We still have a crime to solve. So, fetch the clue board."

"Fetch?" I chuckled as I stood up. Grinning at Nikki, I said, "Consider yourself lucky that your familiar is a sweet-tempered golden retriever. Instead of a snarky old witch, now gray tabby cat."

I finished setting up the clue board. It was clearly visible for Nikki and Milo to read. I picked up a piece of chalk. "Alright, I think we're ready. First, I wanted to share that Petra's room at the B & B seemed to have a heavy weight to the space. Do you know how you can feel tension when you walk into a room where people are arguing? It was like that, only without humans present."

"Residual energy," Milo said. "It can happen with non-magicals too."

I folded my arms over my midsection. "I'm going to print the pictures on my phone. Give me a few minutes."

Why I hadn't done that first was beyond me. I hurried into the back room. With a snap of my fingers, I turned on the printer and wirelessly synced my phone with it. With a few taps on my phone, the printer began to shoot out images. While I waited, my cell pinged with a message from Gage.

Canisters contained pepper spray, and no poison was detected anywhere in the rooms.
Thanks for the update. See you at my place later. L...

I tucked my phone in my pocket, and I'd add that tidbit to the board. This was interesting news. Holding the pictures up, I did a cursory glance before walking back into the main room. "Now we're ready." I pinned them around the outside of the board. "Here's what I know. Other than that oppressive feeling when the door first opened, Petra was very tidy except for the top of her desk. Papers were scattered on the blotter. I couldn't see what they were, but I'm optimistic Gage will share those pictures tonight."

Nikki got up and walked closer to the board. "Walk us through each image."

Milo arched his back and settled in. "Start with the first picture you took. It will be like we're walking through the scene with you."

I unpinned the first eight-by-ten and handed it to Nikki. "When the door opened, my eye was drawn to the bed and the small throw pillow in the center. From having spent time at the inn during Nikki's wedding, I knew that it was new. Look closely at the needlepoint. Doesn't it look like a bouquet of Queen Anne's lace?"

Nikki sat down next to Milo and held it up for him to

see. "Too bad it wasn't smell-a-pillow. If it reminded one of a carrot we'd know for sure." She looked up. "That wouldn't matter though. The pillow didn't commit a crime."

"True. What if it was a reminder of what Petra could do given the proper motivation? Gage texted and said the canisters from Chaz, Donella, and Roni's rooms were pepper spray and there was no other evidence of the poison. Although I don't think they're blameless. After all, they were happy to go into the library after it closed to look at the amulet again. If they could have gotten their hands through the hole first, one of them would have taken it."

Milo said, "Remember the good news. My amulet will only reflect what is intended. And if it was theft that wouldn't have killed them. Maybe a good jolt but nothing more serious."

"The pillow is important. I'm not sure why without being able to examine it, but we'll find out." I took down the second image. "Next, look at the corner of the bed. There's a small wooden box sticking out. Almost as if it hadn't been shoved far enough back."

Nikki said, "There isn't much to go on with this picture."

I followed suit with each image and gave my assessment. The final picture I handed to Nikki was of a cardboard box. "I can't wait to ask Gage what was in this box. I wanted Dax to open the box from where we stood, but that would be pushing him too far. Besides, when I saw it, Sharon and Mac came bounding up the stairs."

"So where do we go from here?" she asked. "Are we going to have dinner tonight to review all the clues?"

"That's my plan." I saw Sharon coming down the street. "Maybe we can find out a few details sooner." I hurried to the door and stepped onto the brick sidewalk. Giving her a wide smile I said, "Sharon, got a minute?"

She narrowed her eyes and tipped her head in her cautious cop manner. "I'm on my way to grab a late lunch from the café. Do you want to walk with me?"

Behind my back, I gave Nikki a thumbs-up and fell into step beside her. "I'm sure you're wondering what I was doing standing in the doorway of Petra's room."

With a snort, she said, "Not really. Since I've moved to Pembroke Cove, you have a way of worming your way into every murder investigation. Actually, you've become a pretty good amateur sleuth. But if you tell Gage that, I'll deny it."

I laughed to myself at the compliment. Sharon Peabody was a by-the-book kind of police officer, and she was excellent at the job too. "Thank you. But I was wondering if you found anything interesting that might help me, help Gage, and the team."

She gave me a quick side eye. "That took under three minutes for you to get right to the point. Are you sure you're not a cop masquerading as a bookstore owner?"

I chuckled out loud. "Trust me. One cop in my family is enough." Taking a quick gulp of air, I said, "Sharon, please tell me you found something important?"

She stopped and looked around. Grabbing my arm, she pulled me across the street into the town square and strode to an empty bench that was in the open. "Against my better judgment, I'm going to give you the highlights. Because I know you, Lily. If I don't, you're going to go back to the B &

B and somehow find trouble. Hopefully, this will be enough to have you steering clear."

I nodded. Finally, good information was about to flow my way.

"We found glass cutting equipment."

"Was that in the wooden box under the bed?"

Her brow quirked. "You're very observant. Maybe you should tell me what you saw, and I'll fill you in on what I can."

I rubbed my hands together and smothered the grin that wanted to bust out from my insides. This was good stuff. "There was an embroidered pillow of Queen Anne's lace that shouldn't have been in the room. The wooden box. A cardboard box under the desk and the top of the desk looked as if it had been rifled through. You know, as if someone had been looking for something and got interrupted before they could tidy it up again. Everything else looked as I would have expected."

Her eyes widened briefly as she shook her head. "How do you do that? All you did was stand in the doorway." She narrowed her eyes and leaned closer to me. "Please tell me you didn't enter the room and touch anything?"

I took in a deep breath and held it in, quickly counting to ten. When I exhaled, I gave Sharon a pointed look. "Do you really think I would break my word or contaminate a crime scene? Sadly, this isn't our first murder in town."

With a brisk nod, she said, "I'm sorry. For my own peace of mind, I had to ask."

Clasping her arm to reassure her I said, "I get it. But what can you tell me?"

With another visual sweep of the area, she slid closer to me. "Of course this is confidential, but I know Gage and Dax will share everything with you tonight. Since I'm assuming we're gathering for dinner."

"Yes, we'll meet at my place around six as usual." I gave her an encouraging nod as my pulse rate kicked in.

"Like I said, the glass cutting equipment was in the wooden box. We found two small canisters tucked into the pillow, contents unknown at this point."

My hand flew to cover my heart. "Please tell me you had gloves on?"

"Gage had us go in with face masks, too. He wanted us to be very careful, and we both changed clothes the minute we got back to the station. Just to be on the safe side."

I exhaled. Glad to hear that everyone was taking this seriously. "What about the desk?"

"From what I could tell, it was notes for a proposal she was working on. It referenced Heart of the Soul, but the interesting part, she only listed her name. Dr. Beale wasn't listed as a co-author. From what he said, I thought they worked on it together."

"They were, but I think she kept him as the silent partner, and she was the superstar."

"Huh. Wouldn't that give him a stronger motive for silencing her?"

I leaned against the bench. "I was just beginning to give him the benefit of the doubt, but he has to be the killer. He may have gotten tired of being on the fringe of greatness, especially with such an important project such as the amulet."

"I don't get it. What is so special about that particular piece?"

I chewed the inside of my cheek as I wondered what was the best way to answer the question. "The history surrounding the Heart of the Soul amulet is that it once belonged to a powerful witch who did not harm anyone or anything. Until it became cursed and then whoever wore it would die. For generations it's been hidden to protect everyone, until now. My guess is the lure of the backstory was irresistible to Petra and the others. In addition, the gems are rare and the piece is stunning."

The color drained from her face. "Do you think there is any truth behind the story? About the witch and the curse?"

"What do you think?" I clasped my hand over hers, and despite the warmth from the sun, she was shivering. "Sharon, are you okay?"

"I. I. Could have. Died?"

"No. You have a good heart and pure intentions. Curses befall bad people or those who want to cause harm. I promise you were safe."

"How can you be sure? It's not like you're a witch or wizard."

I wrapped my arm around her and drew her close to my shoulder. The normally stoic police officer was scared. "I'm a huge history buff and have read extensively about many topics. I promise you were never in danger."

I felt her nod against my shoulder. "Now, why don't you tell me about the cardboard box. What did it contain?"

She pulled away from me, and it was a relief to see color returning to her cheeks. "Chemistry equipment and baggies of dried herbs. Mac took it to EL for some forensic testing. If I were a betting kind of person, my money would be on those herbs. They were used to make the poison since there were heavy-duty gloves and a respirator too."

I jumped up from the bench. "Let me get this straight. You think Petra created the poison in her room?"

Chapter 20
Lily

Finally, it was the end of the day. Nikki was stopping home to pick up Murphy, her familiar, before going to my house. I locked the door to the store. Milo sat on the sidewalk waiting patiently as so many questions whirled in my brain. There had to be more to the Simon and Petra relationship. He seemed truly upset and almost at a loss with her gone.

"Milo, I need to make a stop before going home. You can wait for me in the car or meet me there, your choice."

His tail flicked from one side to the other. "Why don't I just go with you?"

"It won't take long. I just need to ask Simon a couple of questions since we know that Petra was the one who made the poison and ended up killing herself."

"My dear witch, on several occasions you've promised Gage never to go off by yourself to confront anyone involved with a crime. It sounds like you're about to go back on your word."

"I just need to know how the glass cutter worked in the

circle and does it work the same on plastic? When I looked it up earlier everything on the internet says you need to have access to two sides. But there weren't any shards inside or outside the case. Unless Petra cleaned it up, but the circle was chest height so she couldn't have?"

He nodded. "Those are good questions, but let Detective Cutie or Detective Sweet Tea ask them. We should go home and get ready for dinner. I don't know about you, but I'm starving."

"You go ahead. I'll be right behind you." I adjusted my heavy shoulder bag, which contained my wand, *Practical Beginnings*, my laptop, and, of course, my actual handbag. I walked the short distance to the B & B. I smiled to myself as Milo trotted along beside me. As I entered the inn, a clattering of pans came from the kitchen. The main lounge area was brightly lit. Simon was sitting in an oversized leather chair staring into the empty fireplace. I cleared my throat as I got closer.

He looked up. "What do you want?"

I sat down across from him, and Milo perched on the arm of the chair close enough so I could feel the warmth of his body. "Clarification."

"I told the cops everything I know. Why don't you ask them?"

"I'd like the answers straight from you."

His eyes were dull; his skin had sunk into his cheeks. Sitting in front of me was a defeated man. "Ask your questions and then leave me alone. I can't wait to leave this town and all of this behind me."

I placed my tote bag at my feet and folded my hands in

my lap. "How come there weren't any remnants of the plastic after you cut it?"

He gave me a sharp look. "What makes you think it was me?"

"You're experienced. Petra wasn't."

With a nod, he said, "I found out what her plan was right before she left to go back to the library. She asked to borrow a few tools from my workshop before we came here. I didn't want her to make it worse than it would be, so I said I'd cut the case. And you're right; it's easy if you know how to do it."

"Tell me." I leaned forward not to miss a single word he said.

"You start by scoring the material in a circle, just like you would for making any circle. But the tricky part is adding the score lines, making it look like pieces of pie. Once you've gone over the score lines on the wedges a few times, you can tap out the center using a suction cup, leaving the hole. I was able to do it on the first try. I guess taking the classes helped after all." With a derisive laugh, he said, "Who would have thought a hobby I love would turn into criminal activity?"

"If you knew she planned to steal the amulet, why help her?"

"Have you ever loved someone so much it was all you could think about, but the person never knew how you felt?"

I wasn't about to share my history with Gage and our long friendship where we had loved each other but were afraid to speak up. "That must have been very difficult."

"Petra had become someone I didn't recognize

anymore. She was driven to uncover the truth, not just the Heart of the Soul amulet, but in her mind, that was the ticket to more prestigious opportunities. She'd do anything to get ahead."

"And you would do anything to help her?" My question was gentle but honest.

He nodded. "Not at first. I thought if I became indispensable to her, she'd see me as a partner, not just in work but in her whole life. I thought I could change her back to who she had been when we first met."

"Tell me about the old Petra."

A small smile played over his lips. "She had an amazing sense of humor. Even when we were working long hours, she always found a way to make it fun. A playful gesture, a joke, packing our favorite chocolates for snacks. We liked so many of the same things. I knew we were meant to spend our lives together. But a year ago, she began to forage for herbs and work in the lab by herself. I teased her and asked if she was making love potions. She snapped back that I wished she was. That hurt my feelings but not enough to walk away."

"Why do you think she wanted to make herb blends?"

His head snapped up. "Come on, do you really think she was making a spice blend for cooking? You saw her in action. She had morphed into the worst version of herself. All Petra wanted to do was hobble or incapacitate other archeologists she perceived as competition."

Milo said, "Ask him if he ever helped her forage for the herbs."

Simon gave Milo a cursory look before saying, "Sadly,

she didn't see me as a partner in this project. I was the overeducated gofer."

I was starting to make progress. I slipped my hand into my bag, thought a quick spell to record this conversation, and under my breath said, "And so it shall be."

He said, "Did you just ask me a question?"

"No sorry. I was making a mental note to myself, but did you go with her when she was harvesting her herbs?"

"No. She shut me out." He hung his head and rubbed the back of his neck with his left hand. "I would have done anything with, or for, her."

"Even kill the competition?"

His right hand curled into a fist. "I don't appreciate what you're implying." Simon glared at me.

I eased the chair over the wood floor creating more space between us. In a quiet voice, I said, "Simon, I'm asking a question. How far would you go to help her?"

He jumped up, his fists clenched at his sides, and his face went from deep red to almost purple. "I wouldn't kill for her. Yes, I made it easy for her to steal the amulet. Is that something I'm proud of? No! But she died. Now I have to face the consequences of what I have done." Wringing his hands, he began to pace the width of the room.

"Simon, I'm sure Detective Erikson will work with you to minimize the repercussions of damaging the display case. Maybe if you agree to pay restitution and some community service, he can let you off with a warning."

"What about my career? Once it gets out what I did, I'll be ruined. I only wanted Petra to work hard, live by good ethics and morals, and stop taking shortcuts. Could she do that, no." He bumped into a side table sending a lamp crashing to the floor. "Now, look what you made me do."

I paused. Did I go over and help pick up the pieces or let him calm down first?

"Why don't you sit down for a few minutes, and I'll help you clean that up afterward?"

He narrowed his eyes as he stared me down. "So you can grill me some more?"

"I want to help you." I pointed to the chair he had been sitting in. "Join me."

Milo leaned into me. "Are you sure this is a good idea?"

I nodded more to Milo than to Simon. "Come on. You need someone to talk to, and I'm a good listener."

His shoulders sagged as he shuffled to the chair. "What do you think will happen to her work? It was everything to her."

In my heart, the work was the only real connection Simon had to Petra. Without it, he would have to let go of the dream of what he had wanted for a life with her. "You won't write the proposal. You have all her notes, and if she had you as her assistant, she must have thought you were capable."

He gave me a questioning gaze. "Do you really believe that?"

"Brilliant people surround themselves with other brilliant people. You have worked with her for a long time. She wouldn't have kept you around if you weren't more than capable." I was dying to ask him about the canister and what she was doing with a poison-filled atomizer.

He was nodding. "That's true. She always pushed me to read more and learn more, just like with the stained glass. Petra said it would help me when we had to examine artifacts." A slow smile crept to his eyes and he sat up straighter. "Can you call Detective Erikson? There is something he needs to know about the night Petra died."

I could feel my breath quicken. "What do you mean?"

"It's my fault she's dead."

Milo said, "Now would be a good time to throw a protection bubble around us."

Before he finished the sentence, Simon withdrew a small pale green canister from under the seat cushion.

All I had to do was think of the protection spell, and it wrapped around us like a cashmere blanket. "Simon. Stop!" I pulled Milo behind me to put myself between us. There was no way he was getting a second dose if my protection spell wasn't strong enough against a poison.

The door banged open. Gage and Dax rushed into the room. Simon leaped up, holding the canister in front of him. His finger was on the plunger. He pulled off the cap and tossed it aside.

Gage said, "Don't do anything you'll regret Simon."

His arm began to tremble. "It's not what you think. I told Lily I needed to talk to you, and I wanted to show her this."

"Put the canister on the table and slowly move away from it." Gage inched closer.

My heart hammered in my chest. I couldn't allow anyone to get hurt. I glanced at Dax who gave me a reassuring nod. I knew how to extend the protection spell around them, but would it work for a chemical attack?

He grasped Gage's shoulder. "I've got this."

I could see his lips moving, and I could hear what he

was saying, but Gage and Simon didn't seem to. Simon set the canister he had been holding on to the mantel and slid like a wet noodle into the chair. Dax flicked out an evidence bag and a pair of gloves from his back pocket. And within seconds, the danger was behind us. The canister was secured.

Gage dropped to one knee and took my hand. "Are you all right?"

I nodded as the tension slipped from the room.

Simon choked out a sob. "It's my fault Petra's dead."

Dax, Gage, and I turned our attention to him. I asked, "What do you mean?"

He pointed to the bag Dax was holding. "I knew she had done something bad with the pepper spray, and I didn't want anyone to get hurt. I switched the canister she gave me with hers before we went to the library. I've never used the stuff and was planning on tossing this into the garbage when we got back, but I never had the chance. She just had pepper spray. That one is her doctored version."

Milo pushed on my back. "Do you know what this means?"

I put him on my lap and nodded. "Gage, it all just clicked into place. I know what really happened. Part of what Simon is saying is the truth as he knows it."

Now that all eyes were on me, I said, "Petra did create the poison, and I'll bet the canister in that bag is just pepper spray. Do you remember she was wearing the amulet when they all left the library and there was a scuffle? A couple of people had dropped their pepper spray." I said, "Simon did you drop your canister? And did Petra drop hers?"

He nodded. "Mine rolled to my feet. As soon as I picked it up I stashed it in my pocket."

I shook my head. "Petra must have picked up the switched canister. Then she accidentally sprayed herself when she thought she was poisoning everyone else. As soon as she got the spray in her face, the musty odor the concoction gave off was unmistakable. That's why she raced to the ocean to try and wash it off, but it attacked her respiratory system, and by using both the devil's snare and water hemlock, it was lethal. Much quicker than just one of them. Petra died by her own poison."

Milo said, "And wearing the amulet, which causes good or evil to bounce back, she didn't stand a chance."

I watched as Simon's face fell.

"It wasn't your fault. You tried to do the right thing. Sometimes, karma is unavoidable."

He buried his face in his hands. "Greed and ego are what killed Petra."

Dax said, "Its better the truth came out."

He looked to Gage. "Does this mean I'm under arrest for her death? Since someone has to be held accountable."

Gage took my hand. "You should have spoken up knowing what she planned to do, but you didn't kill her. The guilty person has already been held accountable."

I stood and scooped Milo into my arms. "I'm going to head home." I kissed Gage's cheek. "You can finish up here, and I'll see you later."

I touched Dax's arm on the way out the door. Softly I said, "Look after things, will you?"

He winked. "What are brothers for?"

* * *

I finished hanging the last sign on my deck and admired the decorations. Nikki was putting the finishing touches on the cake and other food in the kitchen while Gage set up the drink area at the bottom of the steps. The fire pit was filled with wood for the bonfire later.

With a smile on my lips, I said, "Hi, Dax," without turning around.

"How do you do that?" He hugged me from behind, and I laughed.

"Have you forgotten I'm a witch?"

He drawled, "How could I? I swear we're two witches from the same coven, if you'd been born in Louisiana, that is."

I poked him in the chest as a lump filled my throat. "I'm going to miss seeing you every day."

"Likewise, but I'm only half an hour away, and if you ever learn how to fly, it will be even quicker."

That was an interesting idea. So far, I hadn't been allowed anywhere near a broom. "Well don't be a stranger. Act like the brother you've become. Don't forget you have an important job coming up." I nodded in Gage's direction. "Best man."

He gave me a long look. "Are you ready to set the date?"

"Not quite yet but almost. I love being engaged, and we'll start making changes to the house next month so we'll be more comfortable."

I pointed to the sign. "What do you think?"

"Congratulations, Chief Peters." He laughed, "It has a nice ring to it, right?"

"It does. After all we've been through a lot lately with the archeologists and the traveling museum exhibit finally leaving. Life is returning to normal, and it's time to celebrate." I threw my arms around him and held him tight. Blinking away the tears that clung to my lower lashes, I said, "You've become one of my dearest friends and brother. Don't think you can forget about me."

He kissed my forehead. "Ditto."

I heard the rasp in his voice and understood. It was all that could be said for now. "Why don't you help Gage before everyone arrives?"

"Lily Michaels, you're one of the best people I've ever met. I can't wait for my next adventure in Robin's Pointe, but you and I will always be connected. A great witch is emerging, and I can't wait to continue to be a part of your life."

I gave him a little shove. "Stop before you make me cry."

Gage ran up the steps and slipped an arm around my waist as he shook Dax's hand. "Hey, you two, no crying at a going away party."

Dax slipped his arm around my waist on the other side and clapped a hand on Gage's shoulder. "Who would have thought this is where the chapter would end?"

I gave both men a sassy wink, and Milo hopped up on the table. He said, "Maybe Lily should read *the book* to see what happens next?"

Dax and I laughed, and Gage looked at Milo. "Did you just tell Lily to read her book?"

Milo bowed his head.

Gage threw back his head and yelled, "*YES!* I finally understand Milo."

I squeezed Dax and kissed Gage. "I know how this story will continue. We'll live our best lives as a family."

If you loved Artifacts & Amulets help other readers find this book: **Please leave a review now!**
Are you ready to read more from the Lily and the gang in Pembroke?
**Keep reading for a sneak peek at
Cranberries & Criminals
A Book Store Cozy Mystery Series
Order Now
Or
Shop at Lucinda Race**

Not ready to stop reading yet? If you sign up for my newsletter at www.lucindarace.com/newsletter you will receive an excerpt for Cookies & Capers, the introduction of when Lily met Milo right away as my thank-you gift for choosing to get my newsletter.

Cranberries & Criminals

A
BOOK STORE
COZY
MYSTERY

Book Nine

LUCINDA RACE

Chapter One

Lily

I hurried through the town green taking the shortcut from my bookstore to my favorite bakery, the Sweet Spot. Well, the only one in my charming town of Pembroke Cove. The crisp air tingled my nose as I inhaled, pulling the cold November air deep into my lungs. Despite the sun climbing in the bright blue cloudless sky, I pulled the collar of my jacket closer to my chin. Waiting on the sidewalk outside the shop was my best friend and fellow witch, Nikki. I drew closer and she greeted me with a grin.

"Hey, Lily." She gave me a quick hug. "Thanks for getting me out of my kitchen. I've been rushing to finish my frozen pies that are on pre-order for Thanksgiving. I can't believe how many people want to bake off their pies so they'll be freshly baked this year, but it makes it easier for me."

Nikki was an amazing baker and supplied most of the restaurants up and down the coast with desserts as well as specialty products like wedding cakes and holiday pies.

Chapter One

Me? On most days I had trouble boiling water. "I'm just glad you're up for coffee, and William has the magic touch when it comes to the cinnamon pecan buns that I can't get enough of."

She laughed and pulled open the heavy glass door. "That's the one thing I'll never even think of trying to make. No one could ever bake them like William."

I walked inside and, for a moment, closed my eyes, letting the smell of yeast, sugar, and cinnamon wrap around me like a cozy blanket while my mouth watered. The display case caught my eye. I audibly groaned and grabbed her arm. "Nikki, he has the buns but also chocolate croissants." I patted my midsection and thought of my fiancé Gage Erikson. We were close to setting a date for our wedding. If I added to my curves, who knew if I'd be able to wear my mom's dress?

She leaned over my shoulder. "I know what you're thinking. You'll look beautiful on that special day. I promise."

Giving her a playful swat, I asked, "How do you do that?"

"For as long as we've been best friends, how could we not know what the other is thinking on most days."

I flashed her a grin. "True." A paper pinned to the corkboard above the coffee urns caught my attention. "What's that?" Crossing the short distance, I read out loud, "Cranberry Bake-Off."

Nikki came up behind me. "It's for amateurs. You should enter. I can teach you how to make muffins or something easy before next Friday. It would be fun to see you stretching out of your comfort zone."

With a snort, I said, "This last year, I've been like a rubber band. Learning to be a witch from my snarky familiar has been a challenge. Toss in a few murders I helped solve, and I've been busy. Who's had time to learn to bake?" I gave her a side-eye. "Too bad one of my witchy skills wasn't in the kitchen." She knew I was referring to her particular specialty.

With a huge smile that showed off her pearly whites, she said, "We can't all be a kitchen witch. In fact, it's more rare than you think. Besides, you have skills I don't. The spell you cast with Dax to discover the secrets of the Heart of the Soul amulet, now, that's something I could never have done."

With a shrug, I said, "I guess that's what makes our coven so special. We're all different."

"Ladies," William came up behind us. "I see you've read the announcement. And forgive me, I couldn't help but overhear your conversation. Nikki's right, Lily. You should enter. I'd be happy to give you some tips, too. Cranberries are fairly easy to work with as long as you have enough sweetness to balance the tart."

Clasping my hands in front of me, I chewed the inside of my lip. Why couldn't I try my hand at baking? It wasn't like anyone would die from eating a muffin at a baking competition. Who knows, maybe I could surprise Gage by cooking something so he wouldn't have to be the primary chef after we tied the knot. I tapped my chin and scanned the poster again. "It says there are three rounds. I'm guessing that means the recipes will be more difficult with each round. I'd be thrilled if I made it through the first elimination."

William squeezed my shoulder reassuringly. "Lily, I've known you a long time. You can do anything you set your mind to. But remember, for this competition, there's no witchcraft. It has to be all non-magical. It's the only way it would be fair."

I patted his hand. "Even if you give me a few pointers, and Nikki too, I don't think I have a chance, but I'm willing to try."

"That's the spirit," he said. "Now I'll give you the sign-up sheet, and you can fill it out before you leave the shop." With a wiggle of his eyebrows, he said, "Plan on coming by tomorrow morning around eight. We'll have our first lesson in reading a recipe and correctly measuring ingredients."

Nikki draped her arm around my other shoulder. "I'll swing by your place tonight, and we'll practice by baking cookies."

The smiles on their faces didn't hide their excitement.

My mouth went dry, and my voice croaked as I said, "Will they give me the recipes or a cookbook to follow?"

William frowned. "I hadn't thought of that. Nikki, we should choose several easy recipes that Lily can print out. I suspect most of the competitors will be experienced and create something off the top of their heads."

Her forehead wrinkled, and she paused before nodding. "Good idea."

For the second time, a shiver of nerves raced up and then down my spine. "You're making this sound more intimidating than facing down someone who's trying to kill me."

Nikki laughed. "Not at all. Between William and me,

we'll have you ready to measure and mix with the best bakers in the county."

I knew she was being sweet. Nikki had seen some of my past baking disasters firsthand, but to William's point, I had been doing all kinds of things I would never have dreamt possible. With a deep exhale, I said, "I'm going to do this with your help. Before we even start to contemplate what comes next, I'm going to need sustenance—at least one cinnamon pecan roll and maybe even cookies to go with an extra-large coffee."

Being the best friend ever, Nikki said, "My treat, and let's not forget two chocolate croissants."

The sun was low in the sky, and it bathed my store in a golden light. I flopped into the wingback chair at the front of my shop. A whoosh escaped my lungs. "Nikki, how do you do this baking thing? Learning a spell is a snap compared to picking out recipes that I might be able to bake. And I use the word *might* with great reverence."

She closed the cookbook in her lap. Since I had to bake as a non-magical, we decided to scour cookbooks for recipes instead of the way Nikki baked with the combination of magic and hands-on experience. With a wink, she said, "The best way to do anything well is to read the book."

I groaned. "Now you sound like Milo. Speaking of which, I wonder where the gray fur ball is snoozing." I got up and wandered around the shop, checking all his favorite napping zones. Finally, I saw the tip of his gray bushy tail lazily sliding from left to right over the carpet in the children's section. I knelt on the floor and peered under a little wooden chair. Reaching in, I ruffled the fur on his back.

In his typical kitty grumble, he said, "Go away. Can't you see I'm sleeping?"

My face split into a wide grin. "You're not, you're talking to me. Besides you can't sleep the entire day away. What if I needed your help?"

He rolled to his side and looked at me through slits in his deep green eyes. "Do you?"

"As a matter of fact, yes. Join me and Nikki out front. I have news."

He lifted his head, and his eyes opened wider. "Another murder investigation? We've been in a nice groove lately; no one's bit the dust since Petra Addington."

"For once, I'm not trying to solve a murder." Milo was right; things had finally returned to a normal, sleepy town after we had eight suspicious deaths in the span of eighteen months. Coincidentally, the spate of murders and deaths had started when I discovered I was a witch. Not that I thought the events were related to each other.

I got up from the floor, brushed my hands on my jeans, and said, "Milo, come on out. Please."

Being a familiar came with certain expectations between a witch and her familiar. But my bond with Milo was far beyond what I had ever expected. He was my right hand, always ready to help me with anything, and that included the occasional human-interest puzzle as I liked to think of my part in solving crimes.

"Has Detective Cutie dropped by the shop today?"

I smiled as he used Gage's special nickname that few witches knew about. "No. With Dax moving to Robins Pointe, he's been extra busy. There's a new rookie cop, and training has fallen to Gage."

Chapter One

"That's right, I forgot about Peabody and Mac being promoted to detective." He crawled on his belly out from under the low-sitting chair and did a downward-facing dog stretch before moving into an arched-back cat stretch. He tipped his little head to the side and gave me a contemplative look. "How long are you going to hold me in suspense with this big news?"

I clasped my hands behind my back and rocked on the balls of my feet. "Not until you come out front."

He narrowed his eyes. "You are an exasperating witch. I wonder if I can appeal to the coven for a new one?"

"Ha. That's doubtful. You've said on more than one occasion we're connected forever."

"Don't remind me." He sat back on his haunches and swiped his paw over his face.

I bent over and scooped him into my arms. "Stalling time is over."

When I returned with Milo, Nikki put aside the cookbook she had been reading and said, "Where have you been hiding, little man?"

If a familiar could do a haughty sniff, it would be mine. "For your information, napping and hiding are not the same thing. If I had been doing the latter, Ms. Witch would never have found me."

I placed him on the upholstered chair. "Now, for my big surprise." I rubbed my hands together, trying to muster more enthusiasm than I felt. "I've entered a baking competition for next weekend. I would like your help in selecting a few recipes to have ready to bake. With some practice, I could possibly win this event."

"Wait. What. You. Bake?" He glared at Nikki. "You're encouraging this insanity. If anyone was going to enter, it should be you, and that win would be a lock."

Nikki said, "This is for nonprofessionals, and I happen to support Lily's attempt at broadening her skills in the kitchen."

"You'd better see what spells you can learn from *Practical Beginnings*."

He always resorted to bringing up my family's book of magic. "Milo, I have to do this the non-magical way, which is why I need your support. Now, we've selected several recipes. I'd like for you to take a look at what we have so far for muffins, cookies, cake, and even bread. Do you think they all sound good?" I took the stack of open cookbooks and held each one up for Milo to peruse. Thank the stars he could read. I didn't have to explain it all to him.

He snickered and murmured under his breath how there were some witches who should stay out of the kitchen except when opening a can of tuna and best suited to calling for takeout.

Tapping my foot while he took his sweet time, I wanted to remind him rude comments weren't needed. Instead, I chose to ignore his snark. He had to finish reading. To his credit, he nodded at a page in each book and only shook his head once. By the time I got to the final cook book, he had selected one of each variety.

After setting the last book aside, I said, "For the record, smarty pants, I have a few signature dishes that you've never complained about— roast chicken, fish, and scrambled eggs."

He nodded. "True, and Lily, I'm not complaining,

much. You have other talents that Nikki doesn't have. Cooking just isn't your thing. The idea of you entering a baking competition has caught me off guard. As always, I'll do whatever is needed to support you." His tail swished from side to side. "And if by some quirk of fate, you do win, I'm expecting that very nice smoked salmon from Betty's Market. It will be adequate compensation for my assistance." He hopped from the chair to the floor. "When do lessons begin?"

"As soon as I close the shop. Nikki's coming over, and later Gage and Steve will be around for dinner." Nikki smiled when I mentioned her new husband. It still didn't seem right not to include Dax Peters in that statement. He was our friend and witch, who was more like family and formerly of Pembroke Cove. As of a few months ago, he was hired as the chief of police in Robins Pointe and was missed terribly when we got together for these impromptu meals.

Milo said, "I, too, miss Detective Sweet Tea."

I couldn't help but smile at Milo's nickname for Dax. "Hopefully, he can get away in the next few weeks and join us for some holiday cheer."

"If Nikki's baking, I'm sure he'll be around. That witch has a sweet tooth." He stalked from the room and, over his shoulder, said, "I'll see you at home."

I sank into the chair that Milo had vacated and gave Nikki a long look. "I know you encouraged me, but do you think I'm crazy for entering this contest? Milo's right. Even before I knew I was a witch, the kitchen was my least favorite room in the house."

She leaned forward and clasped my hand. "I know

Gage does most of the cooking, but wouldn't it be nice to bake muffins or a pie for your handsome fiancé if you had the confidence to do it?"

I pointed to the stack of cookbooks we hadn't looked through yet. "Maybe we should find a couple of more recipes just to have enough flexibility for the contest."

She handed me a thick volume from off the stack.

"Nikki, please tell me you'll come to the event. I know we can't use magic, but with you in the room, it will be the moral support I need."

"Ogres couldn't keep me away." She squeezed my hand. "Gage, me, and everyone you love will be there cheering you on."

I hugged the cookbook to my chest and got up. With a sigh of determination, I said, "Well then, with everyone I love there, I'd better learn how to crack eggs without getting shells in the batter and cream butter, and I need to remember to include the cranberries."

To order click here:
Cranberries & Criminals
A Book Store Cozy Mystery Series
Order Now
Or
Shop at Lucinda Race

A Free Story for You

Have you enjoyed Artifacts & Amulets? Not ready to stop reading yet? If you sign up for my newsletter at www.lucin darace.com/newsletter you will received Cookies & Capers which is the start of Lily and Milo's adventure as my thank-you gift for choosing to get my newsletter.

Cookies & Capers

I stood in front of the old wood and glass door as I pock-eted the keys to the Cozy Nook Bookshop. Aunt Mimi had signed her bookstore over to me. She said it felt like giving me her baby. But I loved the shop as much as my aunt did. We had worked together for the last twelve years. After attending the University of Maine, I had a degree in history and education. I had always wanted to be a teacher, but jobs were scarce and after substituting for a few years, I moved back to my hometown of Pembroke, Maine, and Aunt Mimi hired me as soon as I unpacked my suitcase.

Spending time with my aunt, learning the business, had

been the best experience. I offered to buy the shop when she wanted to retire, but she wouldn't hear of it. As long as she had free books for life, and her long-term boyfriend Nate, she said it was a fair deal. From my point of view, I had built-in backup for years to come.

Now that I was the bookshop owner, Aunt Mimi was no longer coming in every day which meant her cat, Phoenix, wasn't either and the space felt empty without a kitty lying in the window or skulking about as kitties do. I was off to the Pembroke Animal Palace to see if I could find a match.

It was a short walk in the bright noonday sun. The spring air from the ocean carried a tang of salt, but the breeze was refreshing. I waved to one of my best friends, Gage Erikson, as he drove past in his police-issued sedan. My heart fluttered in my chest.

He was a detective on the force. Not that we had much crime in our small seaside town. But one of these days I was going to get brave and tell him I had been carrying a torch for him since we were in ninth grade. What's the worst thing that could happen? We'd still be best friends, right?

I continued down the brick sidewalk, waving to William North from the Sweet Spot Bakery. He was sweeping the area around the small bistro tables in front of the bakery. William was wearing a large pristine white apron and a wide smile. A deep inhale confirmed my suspicion. He was baking cookies. My mouth watered. I did a half turn and went back to where he was finishing up. "Good morning, William." I bobbed my head in the shop's direction. "What is that tantalizing smell?"

He held open the brightly polished glass door. "One of

your favorites, Lily. Chocolate chip and pecan cookies. Can I interest you in one before you continue on your mission?"

I gave him a side-look. "Mission?"

He chuckled. "Over the years my Lulu had said you had two speeds, strolling and purposeful. Just now it was purposeful so hence you're on a mission."

"I'm going to the shelter, hoping to find a kitty. The shop is lonely now that Phoenix is home every day with Aunt Mimi, and I think a cat napping in the window adds an air of serenity to the place."

"Unless you're allergic."

He had a point, but I was not willing to be deterred. I smiled. "I'm always happy to deliver to a customer." I leaned over the glass bakery case, like a kid pressing her nose against the candy case. "You made sugar cookies too and frosted them?" I sighed. I was going to need to exercise more if he continued to bake all my favorites. He was smiling at me as I looked up. "Are the chocolate pecan ready?"

He wiggled his eyebrows. "I have a tray cooling in the back."

"Then can I have one of those and a sugar cookie, but to go?"

With a flick of his wrist, he snapped open a white bakery bag and called over his shoulder. "Jerilyn, would you please bring out the last batch of cookies?"

I heard a muffled, coming, and smiled. "It's good that Jerilyn stayed on." I said nothing about his beloved wife Lulu. Rumor had it she was ill and not doing well.

He nodded. "It is. She's a hard worker and excellent with the customers."

Jerilyn bustled in from the back room carrying a large stainless-steel tray. It was lined with parchment paper and cookies the size of the palm of my hand. It was going to taste so good with a hot cup of tea later.

William put two in the bag, along with two sugar cookies, and then he handed it to me. I paid for my cookies and thanked him. "Stop by the shop later. You might just get to meet my new fur baby."

"Sounds like a plan." He grinned and crossed his arms over his rounded midsection. "You're more like your aunt than you realize. Ever since she opened that bookshop, she's had a cat, too."

I paused, tucked the bakery bag in my tote, and with my hand on the door, I turned and gave him a wide grin. "And now it's time I carry on the tradition." With a jaunty wave, I called, "Wish me luck."

Cookies & Capers is only available by signing up for my newsletter – sign up for it here at <u>www.lucindarace.com/newsletter</u>

Love to Read?

**All ebooks and signed paperback copies can be ordered from my website at:
Shop at Lucinda Race**

Cozy Mystery Books

A Bookstore Cozy Mystery Series

Books & Bribes

It was an ordinary day until the book of Practical Magic conked Lily on the head causing her to see stars. And then she discovered her cat, Milo, could talk.

Catnaps & Crimes

The fun continues as Lily practices her magic and needs to investigate another murder.

Tea & Trouble

A fall festival, reading tea leaves and a few clues propel Lily into a new murder investigation.

Love to Read?

Scares & Dares
*What goes wrong at a haunted house is anything but
expected until Lily starts following the clues.*

Holidays & Homicide
Can Lily solve a murder before it ruins the holidays?

Leprechauns & Larceny
Will a dead leprechaun take the shine off the wedding?

Magicians & Murder
When four magicians roll into town for a show more than
fun is on one person's mind.

Artifacts & Amulets
Milo has been keeping secrets, which can be deadly.

Cranberries & Criminals November 2024
Whose half-baked idea was it for bookstore owner and
witch Lily Michaels to enter an amateur baking contest in
her small town of Pembroke Cove, Maine?

Cowboys of River Junction
Second Chances in Montana
*Twenty years later Renee and Hank are back where they fell
in love but reality is like a spring frost and is a long-distance
relationship their only option for their second chance?*

Stars Over Montana
*The cowboy broke her heart but he never stopped loving her.
Now she's back ready to run her grandfather's ranch...*

Love to Read?

Hiding in Montana
Can love flourish while danger lurks in the shadows?

<u>Moonlight Over Montana</u>
From the smoldering ash, she realizes he's all the family she and her daughter need.

The Sandy Bay Series
<u>Sundaes on Sunday</u>
A widowed school teacher and the airline pilot whose little girl is determined to bring her daddy and the lady from the ice cream shop together for a second chance at love.

Last Man Standing/Always a Bridesmaid
<u>Barrett</u>
Has the last man standing finally met his match?

<u>Marie</u>
Career-focused city girl discovers small town charm can lead to love.

The Crescent Lake Winery Series
<u>Breathe</u>
Her dream come true may be the end of his...
Crush
The first time they met was fleeting; the second time restarted her heart.
<u>Blush</u>
He's always loved her but he left and now he's back...the question, does she still love him?
<u>Vintage</u>

Love to Read?

Sweet with a touch of heat holiday romance novels.

It's Just Coffee Series
<u>The Matchmaker and The Marine</u>
She vowed never to love again. His career in the Marines crushed his ability to love. Can undeniable chemistry and a leap of faith overcome their past?

The MacLellan Sisters Trilogy
<u>Old and New</u>
An enchanted heirloom wedding dress and a letter change three sisters lives forever as they fulfill their grandmothers last request try on the dress.
<u>Borrowed</u>
He's just a borrowed boyfriend. He might also be her true love.
<u>Blue</u>
Will an enchanted wedding dress work its magic one more time?

The Loudon Series

<u>Lost and Found</u>
Love never ends... A widow who talks to her late husband and her handsome single neighbor who has secretly loved her for years.
<u>The Journey Home</u>
Where do you go to heal your heart? You make the journey home...
<u>The Last First Kiss</u>
When life handed Kate lemons, she baked.

Social Media

Follow Me on Social Media

Like my Facebook page
Join Lucinda's Heart Racer's Reader Group on Facebook
Twitter @lucindarace
Instagram @lucindaraceauthor
BookBub
Goodreads
Pinterest

About the Author

Award-winning and best-selling author Lucinda Race is a avid fan of fiction. As a young girl, she spent hours reading cozy mystery and romance novels and getting lost in the fun and hope they represent. While her friends dreamed of becoming doctors and engineers, her dream was to become an expert at crafting a captivating novel.

As life twisted and turned, she found herself writing nonfiction but longed to turn to her true passion. After developing the storyline for the McKenna Family Romance series and the Paranormal Cozy Nook Bookstore Series, it was time to start living her dream. Her fingers practically fly over computer keys. She weaves paranormal cozy mystery stories and romance with guaranteed happily ever afters.

Lucinda lives with her two little dogs, a miniature long hair dachshund and a shitzu mix rescue, in the rolling hills of western Massachusetts. When she's not at her day job, she's immersed in her fictional worlds. And if she's not writing mystery, suspense or romance novels, she's reading everything she can get her hands on.